Fragments of a Killer

Walter Moon

Published by Walter Moon, 2024.

This is a work of fiction. Similarities to real people, places, or events are entirely coincidental.

FRAGMENTS OF A KILLER

First edition. November 2, 2024.

Copyright © 2024 Walter Moon.

ISBN: 979-8227749888

Written by Walter Moon.

Also by Walter Moon

The Clock's Secret: Every Tick Tells a Tale
Where Secrets Sculpt the Wind: A Psychological Thriller
Flesh and Fractures: The Soul's Descent into Darkness
Beyond the Scream: She's Crying for Help
The Silent Divide: A Chasm of Secrets and Betrayal
The Haunted Frequency: Echoes of the Damned
The Phantom Agenda: The Curse Behind the Truths
When Identities Collide: The Haunted Doppelganger
Lullabies of the Wicked: The Witching Child
Midnight in the Forest: The Girl Who Bewitched
Sorrows of the Moonlit Witch
The Girl With The Twisted Spellbook
Sketches of a Nightmare: A Witch Girl's Grimoire
Fragments of a Killer

Fragments of a Killer

CONTENTS:-

1. **The First Whisper**
   Introduction to the protagonist, a troubled detective with a dark past, receiving an anonymous tip about a series of murders.
2. **Echoes of the Past**
   Flashbacks reveal the detective's history and a personal tragedy that haunts them, influencing their approach to the case.
3. **The Gallery of Shadows**
   The detective investigates the crime scene: an abandoned art gallery—each victim's death tied to a piece of art.
4. **Portraits of the Dead**
   Discovering the connection between victims leads to unsettling revelations about their lives, motives, and secrets.
5. **A Mind Unraveled**
   The detective's mental state begins to fray as nightmares resurface, blurring the line between reality and hallucination.
6. **The Conspirator**
   An unexpected ally, a forensic psychologist, enters the picture, offering insights into the killer's psyche.
7. **The Game Begins**
   The killer sends a taunting message, challenging the detective and escalating the psychological warfare.
8. **Threads of Deception**
   Clues lead to false suspects, revealing deeper layers of intrigue and manipulation within the victims' lives.
9. **In the Killer's Shadow**

The detective begins to feel the strain as they realize they are being watched—paranoia sets in.

10. Beneath the Surface
Delving into the art world, the investigation uncovers dark secrets and a hidden society linked to the murders.

11. Splintered Allegiances
Friendships fray as the detective's obsession grows, leading to a dangerous confrontation with a close colleague.

12. The Masquerade
A charity ball at the gallery becomes the setting for new revelations and an attempt to trap the killer.

13. Requiem for the Innocent
A shocking death at the gala reveals the killer's reach and forces the detective to confront their own fears.

14. Psychological Warfare
The killer targets the detective's loved ones, turning the investigation into a personal vendetta.

15. Fractured Reality
As the detective spirals deeper into despair, they question their own involvement in the nightmare.

16. The Ties that Bind
Connections between the victims and the detective's past create a web of guilt and responsibility.

17. The Unmasking
The detective finally uncovers the killer's identity, but it leads to a moral dilemma tied to their own history.

18. The Last Stand
A tense confrontation becomes a battle of wits, revealing shocking twists about the true motive behind the murders.

19. Shattered Reflections
In the aftermath, the detective faces the consequences of their choices, reflecting on the psychological scars.

20. **Fragments of Truth**
The case resolves, but open-ended questions linger; the detective must determine whether they can move on or if the past will forever haunt them.

Chapter 1: The First Whisper

The chill of the autumn night crept through the half-open window, swirling around Detective Clara Hayes as she stared at the cluttered desk in her dimly lit office. Papers lay scattered, evidence boards pinned with photographs of victims, and a half-empty coffee mug sat forlornly next to a half-written report. The ticking of the clock echoed ominously, a reminder that time was always slipping away—just like the lives that had been lost.

Clara's fingers drummed absently on the desk as her mind wandered to the case files, each one a heartbreaking testament to human darkness. She hadn't meant to dig into the old cases; she had sworn to leave the past behind. But the ghosts of her own history always lingered, whispering warnings in the shadows of her thoughts.

The shrill ring of her phone shattered the stillness, its sound cutting through the heavy atmosphere. Clara picked it up, her heart racing in anticipation. It could be about the new case—the string of murders that had plagued the city for weeks.

"Detective Hayes," she answered, trying to keep her voice steady.

"Clara," came a low, raspy voice from the other end. It was a voice she didn't recognize, one that sent a chill racing down her spine. "I have something you need to hear."

"Who is this?" She felt a mix of apprehension and curiosity creeping over her.

"It doesn't matter who I am. What matters is what I know." The voice dropped to a whisper, and she leaned closer to the phone, urgency sparking her thoughts. "There's more to the recent murders than you're aware of. Look closer. They're connected—every single one of them."

Clara's pulse quickened as she grabbed a pen, poised over her notepad, ready to write down anything that could help. "What do you mean connected? Who are the victims?"

"There are pieces you haven't seen yet. Fragments that paint a picture you can't ignore. Trust your instincts, and you might just find the truth buried in the fragments."

"Wait!" She called out, but the line went dead.

Clara stared at the phone, breathing heavily. Who was this person? And how did they know about the case? Questions ricocheted through her mind as she grabbed the case files once more, desperation igniting her search. There were currently three victims—a young artist, a business executive, and a barista. They seemed to have nothing in common beyond their untimely deaths, but now, doubt flickered through her thoughts like a dying flame.

She shoved the files aside and opened her laptop, the bright screen illuminating her determined face. The hiss of static from a nearby radio filled the silence as she scrolled through articles about the victims. They were all popular figures, well-liked in their circles. But what if there was something deeper, something hidden beneath the surface?

Clara's eyes narrowed as she studied the photos—a kaleidoscope of smiles, laughter, and a visual of lives cut short. They were vibrant, full of promise; it was hard to imagine how someone could wish them harm. But she knew evil thrived in the shadows, often hidden in plain sight.

Flipping through the pages, she noticed a pattern emerge in details that hadn't struck her before: all three had attended the same art exhibit just days before their deaths. Clara sat back, her heart thumping. Was this the thread that could weave them together? She quickly opened a new search tab, hungry for any reference to the exhibit and the artist behind it.

As she delved deeper, the atmosphere in her office thickened with tension. Her phone buzzed beside her, jolting her back to reality. This time, it was a message from her partner, Officer Mark Reyes.

"Got a lead on the exhibit. Meet me at Fisher's Art Gallery ASAP."

The weight of the night pressed heavily on her. She would have to leave the safety of her office, venture into the world outside. But that whispered cautionary voice still tinged her thoughts—the one that warned her about getting too close to the darkness.

Shoving her notepad and files into her bag, Clara felt the familiar rush of adrenaline coat her skin. She was drawn to this darkness, no matter how much she tried to resist. With one last glance at the quiet street below her window, she turned on her heels, stepping into the unknown—and the hunt for the truth.

As she closed the door behind her, the first whispered words still echoed in her mind. A beginning, perhaps, but also a portent of the shadows yet to come.

Chapter 2: Echoes of the Past

The atmosphere inside Fisher's Art Gallery was palpable with tension—a mix of anticipation and unease. As Clara stepped through the arching doorway, the scent of polished wood and paint lingered in the air. The gallery, usually a vibrant hub of creativity, now felt like a crypt, each empty frame echoing with the lives lost within its shadows.

Mark Reyes was waiting by a large canvas, his brow furrowed in thought. He turned at the sound of Clara's footsteps, his expression grave. "You got my message. We need to talk about the connection."

"Right. The exhibit," Clara said, brushing her fingertips along the edge of the canvas. It was a striking piece, bold strokes of red splashed against a dark background—an unsettling representation of chaos and anguish. "Tell me what you found."

Mark glanced around to ensure no one was listening before leaning closer. "I spoke with the curator. All three victims were involved in that charity gala a week before their deaths. They were part of a group raised funds for struggling artists. An exclusive circle," he said, his voice low.

Clara nodded, recalling the articles she had read. "But why would anyone want to harm them? They were well-liked... respected."

His gaze turned distant, as if he were searching the recesses of his own mind. "Respect isn't always protective. They may have crossed someone's path. Maybe jealousy. Or... something even darker."

An unexpected chill raced down Clara's spine. She could feel the whispers of her past creeping closer. Memories of her own time in the art world, the vibrant colors splattered with shades of loss, flooded her mind. A different gallery, a different night—everything illuminated by the glimmer of hope that art could foster. But that night had turned into a nightmare, one she still couldn't escape.

"Clara?" Mark's voice pulled her back. "You still with me?"

"Yeah, sorry," she replied, forcing herself to focus. "What else did the curator say?"

"Something unusual caught my attention. This gallery had a specific focus on mental health themes in art. The victims had some connection to an artist, Julian Mercer. The curator hinted he had a troubling past but wouldn't elaborate. Apparently, his work has a following of... obsessed fans."

"Obsessed?" Clara's interest piqued, mingled with a dread she could not shake. "What do you mean?"

"His pieces are intense, cathartic, but also disturbingly personal. Some fans believe they're at a deeper level of understanding him—like it's a transcendental experience. There have been rumors that he lost someone significant, which may have influenced his work."

The name hit Clara like a punch to the gut. Julian Mercer had once been considered a rising star. His art had unique energy, capturing the darkness of the human condition. But his abrupt disappearance from the scene was a mystery she had been curious about. "Where do we find him? Is he exhibiting here?"

"Not anymore," Mark said, his voice tight. "He stepped away from the public eye after his last show. No one seems to know where he is now, but we need to dig further into this."

Clara felt a sense of urgency swell within her. The gallery around them held stories—fragile narratives suspended in time. Her heart raced at the thought of reopening that chapter of her past, but she knew it was necessary. The truth was buried beneath echoes that refused to fade away.

Suddenly, a loud crash resonated from the back of the gallery, making both of them jump. Clara instinctively reached for her gun, her heart pounding. "What was that?"

Mark motioned for her to stay back as he moved cautiously toward the sound. Clara followed closely, her pulse quickening. They rounded a corner where the shadows danced ominously along the walls.

As they approached, they found a fallen display, a shattered glass plate and an assortment of art materials scattered across the floor. A teenage girl stood frozen in shock, her eyes wide. "I—I'm so sorry! I didn't mean to knock it over!"

"It's okay," Clara said, lowering her voice as she assessed the scene. "Just be careful. There's some valuable art back here."

The girl nodded, her face flushed with embarrassment. "I just wanted to see the new pieces. I was going to help clean up!"

Clara crouched to pick up a piece of broken glass, noting the girl's trembling hands. "Are you okay? You look pale."

"I went to the gala... I knew the victims," she whispered, her voice trembling. "They were amazing people."

The weight of the moment hit Clara hard. "What do you know about them?"

"Not much, really. Just that they were all... connected," the girl stammered, her eyes darting around. "Some of us think—no one believes me, but—" She hesitated, swallowing hard. "There are stories about the artist... Julian. They say he might be dangerous. That he's still out there."

Mark stepped closer. "Out where?"

The girl glanced around nervously. "In the shadows. People whisper things... I've seen things. His work—it talks to you. You can feel it. But some wanted to exploit him, and it went wrong. Really wrong."

"Where can we find him?" Clara pressed, the urgency in her voice rising.

"I don't know! He changes places. One day he's here, the next—"

Mark glanced at Clara, a silent understanding passing between them. They needed more than whispers and shadows; they needed a plan.

"Stay safe," Clara said to the girl, trying to reassure her despite the gravity of their discovery.

They turned back toward the main gallery, and Clara felt the echoes of the past pulling her in all directions. Somewhere, hidden among the art, lay the truth she needed to uncover. But with every revelation, she felt the weight of her own history lurking behind her, reminding her that some echoes never truly fade.

Chapter 3: The Gallery of Shadows

The soft glow of overhead lights cast long, distorted shadows across the wooden floor of Fisher's Art Gallery as Clara and Mark made their way back to the main exhibition space. The atmosphere was thick with unease, a palpable tension that wrapped around them like a shroud. Each step felt heavier, burdened by the weight of what lay ahead—both in their investigation and in Clara's own turbulent memories.

"Do you think Julian Mercer could have anything to do with the murders?" Mark asked, breaking the silence as they reached the entrance to the main exhibition room.

Clara glanced at the gallery's vast walls adorned with striking pieces of art—every canvas seemed to radiate emotion, anger, pain, and beauty, all intertwining in a complex dance. "If the victims were tied to him, it's possible. But what's his motive? I need to understand his past, to piece together how he might fit into this."

As they stepped inside, the echo of their footsteps mingled with the whispers of bygone conversations. Clara approached a large painting, one that dominated the far wall—a violent riot of colors that seemed to scream at her, demanding attention. It was titled "Chaos Within," a striking representation of a tormented soul struggling amid darkness.

Each brushstroke seemed like a fragment of a story, a glimpse into someone's unraveling mind. Clara felt the hairs on the back of her neck rise as she recalled the memories of her own past, the chaos that had once consumed her life. She forced herself to focus, pushing back the wave of nostalgia and pain.

"Clara, look at this," Mark called, drawing her away from the painting. He stood before a smaller piece titled "Reflections of the Damned," depicting a distorted figure surrounded by shards of glass. The image felt all too familiar, resonating with the emotions she had tried to bury.

"What do you make of this?" Mark asked, leaning closer to inspect the intricate details.

Clara squinted at the piece, her pulse quickening. "It's unsettling. Julian's work often explores themes of identity and fragmentation—like people are only mere reflections of their true selves. It suggests a deeper understanding of suffering and loss."

"But do you think he suffered enough to hurt others?" Mark pushed.

Her mind raced back to the swirling tales of Julian's past—the whispers of tragedy that had followed him like a dark cloud. "If he lost someone close, it could've twisted his perception of reality. Art can be a means to express pain, but it can also become a tool to manipulate."

Suddenly, an uneasy feeling pricked at Clara's instincts. She turned to the side and caught movement through the crowd of onlookers. A figure stood just beyond the fringes of a throng of art enthusiasts—all eyes glued to a massive installation piece in the center of the room. The figure was cloaked in shadows, their features obscured by the dim lighting.

"Who's that?" Clara whispered, her heart racing.

Mark followed her gaze. "Let's check it out," he said, moving with quiet determination.

As they approached, the crowd began to swell, murmurs filling the air as people whispered and observed the artwork. It was an interactive piece—a labyrinth of mirrors surrounded by flickering lights, each reflection distorting the faces of those who entered. Clara felt a wave of anxiety wash over her as she stepped closer to the figure, the memories of her own life reflecting back at her.

The figure finally turned, and Clara felt her breath hitch in her throat. It was a woman, dressed in black, with intense hazel eyes that seemed to pierce through the illusion. There was something hauntingly familiar about her—a resemblance that clawed at the edges of Clara's mind.

"I know who you are," the woman said, her voice steady but low, almost conspiratorial. "You're Clara Hayes, the detective."

Clara's heart raced. "Do we know each other?"

"I've seen you before," the woman replied cryptically. "In whispers... shadows. You're looking for Julian, aren't you?"

Mark stepped closer, his presence a silent support as Clara felt herself on the precipice of recognition. "Who are you?" she asked, forcing calm into her voice.

The woman leaned closer, glancing around the room as if ensuring no one else could hear. "I used to be part of his circle... a connection you could say. But things went wrong. He's not right anymore. You need to be careful."

"Why?" Clara pressed. "What do you know about the victims?"

The woman's gaze turned steely, and Clara sensed a flicker of fear. "They were drawn to him, just like you. He has a way of luring people in, entwining their stories with his. But those who tread too close often pay the price."

"Price?" Mark inquired, his body tense beside Clara.

"The price of desperation. Some seek to understand... others to possess," she whispered, her expression grave. "And those who oppose him—those who threaten to reveal—often don't come back from the abyss."

Clara felt the weight of the woman's words sink into her bones. A chill ran down her spine as memories of her own struggles resurfaced—dangerous paths walked for the sake of art, beauty, and the maddening darkness it unmasked. A flicker of empathy ignited within her; she understood the allure of creation and the consequences it can have.

"Where can we find him?" Clara asked urgently.

The woman hesitated, her expression softening momentarily. "You must tread carefully. He's hidden within the gallery of shadows, and to truly find him, you must understand your own darkness."

Before Clara could respond, the woman turned and melted back into the crowd, leaving Clara and Mark standing amidst the swirling faces of art enthusiasts and the chilling weight of unanswered questions.

"What just happened?" Mark breathed, glancing around for signs of the mysterious woman.

"I don't know, but I have a feeling we're being drawn into something far darker than we anticipated," Clara replied, her mind racing. "We need to find Julian, and we need to do it quickly."

As they stepped back, the gallery walls seemed to pulse with untold stories, each piece a fragment of a deeper truth. Clara's heart pounded in rhythm with the echoing questions in her mind. What shadows had they unleashed by seeking this elusive artist? What fragments of terror awaited them in their pursuit of the truth?

The gallery of shadows was vast, and the echoes of the past were closing in, pushing Clara toward an unsettling realization: sometimes, darkness isn't just a place you explore—it's the very essence that resides within you.

Chapter 4: Portraits of the Dead

The harsh fluorescent lights of Clara's office felt sterile, illuminating the remnants of chaos from her previous investigation. The cluttered desk was strewn with photographs of the victims, each face frozen in a moment of life, now irrevocably lost. Clara sat back in her chair, her mind racing as she tried to piece together the puzzle that had started with the enigmatic call and continued to unravel in the wake of the gallery visit.

Three lives, three tragic endings. The barista, the artist, the executive—each seemingly unrelated, yet now inextricably tied together through their last moments. It felt like weaving a tapestry of human existence, but what threads of fate bound them all?

Clara picked up the first photograph, a smiling young woman with sparkling blue eyes and a splash of paint across her cheek—Emma Lang, a 25-year-old artist known for her striking pastel landscapes. "How could someone do this to you?" Clara murmured, tracing a finger over the image. Emma's work had graced several local exhibitions, her talent celebrated by peers and critics alike.

Pushing the photo aside, Clara reached for the second. The businessman, Adam Marsh, stood casually with his arm draped over a friend's shoulder, laughter frozen on his face. He was well-regarded, a pillar of the community with a philanthropic heart. But what secrets might have lurked behind that charming smile? "What were you involved in, Adam?" she whispered, her gut twisting uneasily.

Finally, she picked up the last portrait: Maya Tran, a vibrant barista whose café served as a local gathering spot for artists and intellectuals. Her warmth and energy had drawn people in, but Clara had learned that she had also been harboring her own demons, battling the shadows of addiction.

Clara's chest tightened. The portraits haunted her, but if she wanted to make sense of this, she needed to venture deeper into their lives. What connected these individuals beyond their final breaths? As Clara flipped through her notes, she couldn't shake the feeling that glimpses of their interactions might be the key.

She turned to her computer, hunting for any connections—social media interactions, shared galleries, common friends. Hours passed as she scoured databases and digital memories that the victims had left behind. A web of intertwined lives began to emerge, revealing a vague outline of a larger narrative.

Suddenly, Mark knocked and entered the room, his brow furrowed. "You look deep in thought. Any breakthroughs?"

"Maybe," Clara said, her voice steadying. She turned her laptop toward him, displaying a web of connections she'd come across. "I've compiled a list of exhibitions and events they attended together. Look here—"

Mark leaned in, squinting at the screen. "They all attended a secret artist's retreat last summer," he noted, his finger tracing the lines on the screen. "It was only by invite and hosted by Julian Mercer."

"Of course," Clara muttered under her breath. "They were drawn together, and now they're shadows of what they were." She felt the frustration bubbling inside her. "But what did they uncover at this retreat? What did Julian say or teach that could've turned deadly?"

"There's got to be more to it," Mark said, his eyes scanning the screen. "Someone had to have heard something. We need to find out who organized the retreat."

Clara's mind raced as she traced the names from the list of participants. "I'll follow the leads here. If anyone survived, they might have insight into what happened there."

"Good plan," Mark replied. "I'll reach out to those who knew them, see if anyone has heard from Julian."

Hours later, Clara found herself sitting in a café, the ghost of Maya's laughter echoing in her mind. She felt drawn to the place, the lively atmosphere tinged with nostalgia. It was strange to think that just a few days ago, this very spot had been filled with the buzz of life that now felt like a distant memory.

As she sipped her coffee, she scanned the crowd, hoping to catch someone from the retreat. She scrutinized each face, searching for echoes of Maya's warmth or Emma's artistic flair. Her heart sank as the reality settled in—vibrancy snuffed out, leaving an expanse of gray where color had once existed.

Just then, her phone buzzed, interrupting her contemplations. It was a message from Mark: **"Got a lead. Someone who knows about the retreat. Meet me at the park near the gallery."**

Clara's pulse quickened as she gathered her things and hurried out of the café. The crisp air bit at her cheeks as she made her way through the darkening streets. The park came into view—a small oasis amid the urban sprawl. She spotted Mark seated on a bench, talking animatedly to a young woman with fiery red hair.

As she approached, Clara's instinct kicked in. The woman's demeanor seemed unsettled, glancing around as if she feared being followed. She looked up as Clara closed the distance, her expression shifting to concern.

"Clara, this is Zoe Campbell," Mark introduced, gesturing toward the girl. "She was part of the same retreat. I thought she could help."

Zoe shifted nervously. "Thank you for coming. I-I didn't want to discuss this over the phone," she said, her voice barely above a whisper.

"Tell us what you know," Clara urged, focusing on the young woman who had stepped into the darkness of the past.

Zoe hesitated, biting her lip. "I barely knew Maya and Emma, but Adam... I was friends with him. The retreat was supposed to be a place of healing, but it turned into something else. Julian wasn't as open or supportive as he pretended to be."

"What do you mean?" Mark asked, leaning forward.

"During our time there, he became... possessive. Almost like he wanted to shape us into something that fit his vision. If anyone questioned him or expressed doubts, he turned cold." Zoe glanced around again, her voice shaking. "I've seen the way he reacts to people who challenge him. It's terrifying."

Clara exchanged a look with Mark, their concern growing. "Did anything happen that made you think he could be dangerous?"

Zoe wrung her hands. "One night, we had a group session—Julian encouraged us to share our wounds and pain, but when Maya opened up about her struggles with addiction, he mocked her. He said art should stem from suffering, but if you're weak, it will consume you. The way he looked at her... I felt a chill. Like he wanted to break her."

"Did you say anything?" Clara pressed, her heart racing.

"No. I was scared. I thought if I spoke up, I'd be next," she whispered, her voice trembling. "But after that night, I started noticing subtle changes in Maya. She became distant, like she was lost in his world. At the same time, Adam seemed more protective of her."

"Protective?" Mark echoed. "Did he say anything to you about that?"

Zoe shook her head. "Only that he wanted to help her. But I think things spiraled out of control after that. The last group session before we all left had a different vibe. Julian had a dark, manic energy. He said—" she faltered, a look of terror crossing her face. "He said art was a reflection of the creator's soul. And sometimes... sometimes the soul needs to purge."

Clara felt a wave of realization crash over her; the words echoed in her mind like the stroke of a painter's brush, puncturing through layers of confusion. **A purge.** "Did you see or hear anything else? Anything that would lead to Julian?"

Zoe bit her lip again, clearly distressed. "I left that night. I didn't want to be part of it anymore. I thought I was being paranoid until I heard about the murders. I couldn't believe it—Maya and Emma were gone... Adam too!" She wiped away a tear. "I should have said something. I should have warned them."

Clara felt the weight of Zoe's pain pressing on her heart. "You did the right thing coming here. We need to find him before it's too late."

Mark nodded, resolute. "We'll put together what you've shared. If he's responsible for their deaths, we'll ensure he's brought to justice."

As Clara looked at Zoe, she realized an undeniable truth: the past was never truly buried; it only waited for an opportunity to emerge, twisting lives together in a darkened tapestry. Somewhere among the portraits of the dead lay the key to their resting echoes.

And that key was Julian Mercer.

Chapter 5: A Mind Unraveled

The air in Clara's office felt heavy with anticipation and dread as the darkness of night crept in. The once familiar walls now seemed to pulse with the weight of unanswered questions and the specters of the past. She leaned against her desk, her fingers running absentmindedly over a photograph of Maya, a frozen smile that felt like a distant memory.

Clara had spent hours poring over Lisa's notes, but now they blurred into a haze of information. The web of connections was growing, yet the heart of the matter remained elusive—a disturbing thought gnawed at her. Could Julian Mercer, the artistic mastermind, truly be a killer, hiding behind the façade of creativity?

Her phone buzzed, the sudden vibration breaking through her spiraling thoughts. It was Mark.

"Meet me at the precinct. We've got a lead on a witness."

Clara's heart raced. A witness. Perhaps someone who had been with the victims in their final days. She grabbed her coat and hurried out, the weight of her mission settling on her shoulders like a cold shroud.

The precinct buzzed with activity when Clara arrived; officers hustled, paperwork shuffled. Mark was waiting for her in a small conference room, his expression a mix of excitement and concern.

"Clara, sit. This might change everything," he said, motioning for her to take a seat.

"Who's the witness?" she asked, her pulse quickening.

"Her name is Lila. She was in the retreat group with Maya and the others. She left last minute, but she has insights that could be crucial." Mark leaned forward, urgency in his voice. "She's scared, though. Says she's been receiving threats since the murders."

"Threats?" Clara's breath caught in her throat. "From whom?"

"From someone claiming to be close to Julian. He knows she was going to talk," Mark replied, frustration evident. "The victim's families want answers. We need to provide them, but first, Lila needs to feel safe coming forward."

Clara felt a sinking feeling. "What if she won't come? What if she's too afraid?"

"We'll offer protection. Find her a safe space here, maybe with the witness protection unit. It's the only way," Mark insisted. "But we need to act fast."

They set out to find Lila, their urgency underscored by the ticking clock of impending danger. They made their way to a small apartment complex on the outskirts of town, the building cloaked in a dim light that seemed to mirror the uncertain circumstances. Clara couldn't shake the lingering thoughts of what they might uncover, her instinct intertwining with anxiety.

When they reached Lila's door, Clara knocked gently, her heart pounding in her chest. After a moment, they heard shuffling from inside, and the door creaked open. Lila stood in the threshold, her eyes wide, panic etched across her features.

"Detective Hayes? Officer Reyes?" she asked, voice trembling.

Clara nodded. "Can we come in?"

"Um... sure." Lila stepped aside, her movements shaky as they entered the cluttered space. The living room was dim, shadows lurking in the corners. Clara noticed a flickering candle and scattered art supplies—an unfinished canvas lay face down on the floor, as if abandoned in haste.

"Sit," Mark urged, his tone gentle. "We're here to help."

Lila took a seat on the edge of her worn couch, hands fidgeting in her lap. Clara recognized the raw fear in her eyes, a reflection of her own struggles. "I'm glad you're here. I didn't know who else to trust," Lila said, her voice barely above a whisper.

"We understand this is hard," Clara said, keeping her tone calm. "But we need to hear what you know—whatever you can share about the retreat and what happened afterward."

Lila bit her lip, uncertainty swirling behind her eyes. "I was in the group for a while, but the atmosphere changed after that one night," she said, voice shaky. "Julian became... different. He started prioritizing his own vision over ours, demanding that we dig deeper into our pain. It was like he wanted to expose us, to showcase our worst fears in his art."

"Did something specific happen?" Clara pressed gently, her instincts sharpening as she saw pieces slowly fall into place.

Lila nodded, visibly shaken. "Maya revealed how her addiction was ruining her life, but instead of helping her, Julian twisted it into a mockery. He told her that true art comes from suffering, and that if she didn't expose her darkest moments, she would never find solace. There was this intense energy—everyone was filled with fear."

"What do you mean, fear?" Mark asked, his expression hardening.

"The way he looked at us. It was predatory," Lila recalled, her voice trembling. "He started isolating us, making it seem like only certain voices mattered. Maya's got worse, and I began to see how he fed off her pain."

"Did you see him becoming aggressive?" Clara pressed, emotions swirling inside her.

"Not in the physical sense," Lila said. "But... there was something about his presence. He always hovered, always watching, planting these seeds of doubt. I felt like I was losing my mind just being around him. I decided to leave the retreat, but I was scared. I never wanted to cross him."

"We're here to protect you, Lila," Mark assured her, his voice firm. "Can you tell us when you left? What happened afterward?"

"I left right after the last group session," Lila admitted, her brow furrowing. "I didn't think much of it until the news. I turned my phone off for a couple of days, wanted to avoid trivial chatter."

A knot formed in Clara's stomach. "But when you turned it back on...?"

"I heard about the murders." Lila's voice cracked. "I was horrified, but then the texts started. I thought they were just threats at first, but they warned me... warned me to stay silent about what I knew."

"Who sent them?" Mark pressed.

Lila hesitated, her expression haunted. "I don't know. Just a number. Every night I could feel someone watching me. When I saw news reports about how Maya and the others were connected to Julian, I knew I couldn't stay silent." Her eyes widened as tears spilled over. "I should have spoken out earlier."

"It's not your fault," Clara said, her tone softening. "But we need to act fast. We can protect you, but we need your help. Can you tell us what Julian said about the art?"

Lila nodded, compiling her thoughts. "Julian claimed that the world was divided into creators and destroyers. In his mind, every artist bore a soul that needed to be tested, pushed to limits we couldn't even understand. He framed it as a purging process—if you resisted, if you were caught in the superficial, you met your end."

Clara felt a chill ripple through her. "And if they resisted?"

Lila swallowed hard. "Then he believed their art would never breathe again. He'd eliminate the obstacle in his path. I think... I think that's what happened to Maya, Emma, and Adam. They resisted him."

Mark's eyes darkened. "That's premeditated. That paints a picture of someone who's not just a recluse but someone with intent—someone capable of murder."

A tense silence enveloped the room. Clara felt her breath quickening, adrenaline surging through her veins. They were cornering the truth, the pieces clattering together into a devastating reality. Julian Mercer was not just an artist; he had become a puppet master, his strings interwoven with shadows and pain.

"I want to help you," Lila said, her voice shaking. "But I'm terrified. What if he comes for me?"

Clara reached across the table, gripping Lila's hand gently. "We'll keep you safe. You can stay here at the precinct for now; we have resources." She exchanged a serious glance with Mark. "But we need to move quickly. We have to confront Julian before he strikes again."

As Lila's fear washed over Clara like cold water, the weight of the past seemed to distort her reality. The adrenaline coursing through her veins sharpened her instincts, propelling her forward into the abyss of uncertainty. The fragile line between madness and sanity blurred, and somewhere in the darkness waited Julian—a mind unraveled, ready to unleash chaos.

The hunt had begun.

Chapter 6: The Conspirator

The tension in Clara's office was a living entity, palpable and thrumming. She paced relentlessly, her mind a whirlwind of images and thoughts that refused to settle. The details Zoe had revealed gnawed at her consciousness, illuminating a path laced with shadows. Julian Mercer was no ordinary artist; he was a maestro of manipulation, capable of distorting not just art, but the very souls of those around him.

Mark leaned against the doorframe, arms crossed, studying Clara as she moved like a restless spirit. "You're thinking again, aren't you?" he said, a hint of amusement in his voice attempting to break through the heaviness in the room.

"What if Julian had someone helping him?" Clara stopped abruptly, her mind locking onto a new theory. "What if he had someone in his corner, someone who fed his darker impulses or shielded him from scrutiny?"

"Could be," Mark conceded. "He had a group of devoted followers at that retreat. Perhaps one or more of them might have taken it upon themselves to protect him—or even assist."

Clara's thoughts flickered back to Zoe's words about the group dynamics. "If there was a conspirator, they might have a motive to eliminate anyone who could expose Julian's true nature. Protecting their own interests at all costs."

"Then we need to dig deeper into the people surrounding him. Let's go back to that retreat and see who else was on the guest list." Mark pulled out his phone, pulling up the group email they had discovered during their initial investigation.

As Mark began typing, Clara's eyes drifted to the case board still plastered with images and notes about the victims. Among them were the names of the surviving retreat participants, along with a handful of others in Julian's inner circle. One name repeatedly caught her attention: *Lila Peterson*.

"Mark, look at Lila," Clara said, her voice charged with sudden clarity. "She was an emerging artist before the retreat—known for her evocative portraits and bold themes. There's not much about her after."

"And she was close to both Maya and Emma," Mark noted, scanning his phone. "She might have been aware of Julian's instability and what happened during those group sessions."

"Can you pull records on her? Any recent activity? Social media accounts?" Clara asked, her heart racing at the thought of finding a potential ally—or enemy.

"On it," Mark replied, and soon his brow furrowed in concentration. "There are traces of her online activity, but it's all vague. She hasn't posted in months. It's like she vanished."

Clara's instincts kicked into overdrive. "We need to find her. If she was there, she could still have crucial information about what went on when things spiraled out of control."

As Mark began investigating, Clara felt unease settle in her gut. The evening faded into night, the office illuminated only by the flickering light of the computer screen. As they delved, they uncovered snippets of Lila's past—controversial art exhibits, public disputes with critics, and a tendency to challenge norms.

Finally, Mark found something: "Okay, here's a clue," he said, excitement lacing his voice. "She was last seen at an underground art venue called *The Hive*. It's known for avant-garde expressions and has a reputation for attracting artists on the fringes of the community."

"Do you think she's still there?" Clara asked, her heart racing at the thought of venturing into the darker corners of the art world.

"There's a good chance. It's a popular gathering for artists with unconventional ideas or those seeking refuge from the mainstream. We can try there tonight," Mark suggested, determination clear in his tone.

Clara felt a mix of anticipation and trepidation. They needed answers, but they would be stepping into an environment where danger and creativity intertwined in ways she had always been wary of. Her mind whirled with a thousand thoughts, the tension of the investigation melding with her need for closure regarding the past.

As they exited the station, the cool air enveloped them. Mark's car cut through the quiet streets as they navigated toward the heart of the city. The Hive loomed ahead, its façade an unassuming warehouse that pulsed with life despite the late hour. Colorful murals adorned the exterior, a riot of colors that seemed to beckon to the lost and the desperate.

Inside, the atmosphere was charged—music throbbed through the air, intertwining with the scent of sweat and paint. Pockets of people littered the space, artists and dreamers conversing in low tones, their expressions lit by errant flashes of neon lights. Clara felt alive amidst the chaos, yet the shadows remained palpable, a reminder of the dangers lurking within.

Mark scanned the crowd, focus unwavering. "Where do you think we should start?" he asked, raising his voice to be heard above the din.

"Maybe try the bar first," Clara suggested, squinting through the haze of light and bodies. "People tend to let their guard down with a drink in hand."

They moved through the crowded room, past vibrant displays of art hanging precariously on the walls and installations that stretched the boundaries of creativity. The energy buzzed with unfiltered passion, but a sense of foreboding crept in alongside it.

Mark approached the bar, ordering two drinks while Clara surveyed the crowd, searching for anyone resembling Lila. It felt like a cybernetic dream—everything wrapped in color and swirling possibility. Finally, she spotted a woman standing alone, a canvas bag slung over her shoulder, her auburn hair cascading around her shoulders in tousled waves. She bore the marks of an artist—paint splatters on her clothes and a contemplative gaze that suggested she was lost in thought.

"Lila!" Clara called, stepping forward, hope igniting within her. The woman turned, confusion etched on her face as she caught Clara's eye.

"Who are you?" Lila asked, tilting her head. The wariness was apparent, but there was a flicker of something—curiosity? Fear?

"Detective Clara Hayes. I'm investigating the recent murders, and I believe you may have information that can help," Clara said, rushing to fill the silence, the urgency in her voice demanding attention.

Lila's expression shifted, wariness morphing into something more guarded. "I don't know anything. I don't want to be involved." She began to turn away, but Clara stepped closer, desperation clawing at her chest.

"Please! You were at Julian's retreat. You know what happened, and it's vital. Lives are at stake," Clara pressed, her gaze unwavering. "You don't have to do this alone. There are others who are in danger."

Lila hesitated as the weight of Clara's words sunk in. "I saw things," she eventually admitted, her voice trembling. "Things that terrified me. But I can't... I can't go back there."

"Lila, we're not here to cause trouble. We're trying to stop someone who clearly cannot be trusted," Mark interjected, his voice even. "We can protect you, but we need your help."

She glanced around, each direction filled with people—artists who would support her but also strangers who may not understand. "You don't know what he's capable of," Lila whispered. "It's not just what happened at the retreat; it's what I felt when I was near him. He stirs something in people—an urge to create, yes, but also a darkness that comes alive."

"What kind of darkness?" Clara asked, feeling her heart quicken.

"An obsession. A belief that for beauty to exist, pain must come first. And he..." She shivered, her voice barely audible now. "He's twisted that belief into something dangerous. He's convinced people that their suffering is art, and if they can't endure, they can't create."

Mark shifted closer, creating a bubble of safety around Lila. "If there's a chance he's behind these murders, we need proof. We need to know what you saw."

Lila trembled slightly, glancing over her shoulder, as if sensing eyes watching her. "I might know where he conducts his—sessions," she said, hesitating. "But you have to promise me safety. If he catches wind of this, he won't hesitate to silence me."

"Your safety is our priority," Clara assured her, feeling the weight of the moment settle around them. "Tell us where to find him. We'll handle the rest."

Lila inhaled deeply, fear and courage warring within her. "There's an old studio he uses as a sanctuary. It's hidden away behind the main gallery—an abandoned space where he brings people to create, or... destroy, depending on how you look at it."

"We'll make sure you're safe," Clara promised, locking eyes with Lila. "But we need to move quickly. Time is running out."

As Clara and Mark prepared to leave, Lila's eyes surged with an unspoken plea. They were on the precipice of something much darker than they had anticipated. The line between artist and madman was blurring, and they were stepping into the gallery of shadows, where echoes of the dead lingered—a world where creation could hide a deadly conspiracy, and where Julian Mercer thrived.

Chapter 7: The Game Begins

The persistent rain drummed against Clara's office window, each drop tapping a steady rhythm of urgency into her thoughts. She sat, fingers poised above the keyboard, replaying the recent revelations about Julian Mercer and the unsettling dynamics of the artist's retreat. It felt as though they had unearthed a dark game—one where the stakes were life and death.

Suddenly, her phone buzzed, jolting her from her thoughts. The screen illuminated with a new text message from Mark.

"I think Julian knows we're onto him. Just got an anonymous tip about you."

Clara's heart raced. The walls of her office felt like they were closing in, the shadows lurking like unseen players in this twisted game. How could he know? Had he been watching her, tracking her movements? The unease slithered through her, weaving tighter around her like a noose.

"Meet me at the café. We need to talk."

Clara quickly grabbed her coat and headed out, the rain mixing with the anxiety coiling in her stomach. The café was a short walk, but anxiety turned every step into a mile. As she approached the familiar spot, she spotted Mark seated at their usual table, his brow furrowed, worry etched across his face.

"Clara," he greeted, his voice low as she slipped into the seat opposite him. "You look tense."

"Just got your message. What did the tip say?" she asked, scanning the café as she took a sip of her coffee, searching for any signs of danger lurking in the vibrant atmosphere.

"Someone warned me to keep an eye on you. Said you'd be at this café and that you're digging too deep into things you don't understand," Mark replied, searching Clara's eyes for reassurance.

"Great," Clara said, biting her lip. "What do they mean by things I don't understand? We're just trying to pursue justice for the victims."

Mark leaned closer, his expression grave. "That's the thing, Clara. Julian has a reputation for being charismatic but also dangerously manipulative. I'm worried he could be toying with you. The last thing we need is you becoming part of this twisted narrative."

Clara felt a shiver slice through her. "What does he want from me? I'm a detective—he's the suspect. He shouldn't be able to intimidate me." But deep down, she felt the creeping shadows of doubt.

Mark took a breath, steadying himself. "This could be a game to him. Remember what Zoe said about how he wanted to shape and cleanse his narratives through art? If he sees you as a threat, he might see this as an opportunity to... reclaim control."

The implications of Mark's words hung heavily in the air. "Then we're not just dealing with a murderer; we're playing against a master manipulator. If he thinks he can outsmart us, he'll escalate."

"Exactly," Mark replied. "We need to approach this carefully. Lay low, gather evidence, and cut off avenues of attack. I've sent out requests to the contacts we have; we should get more information about Julian's whereabouts and past interactions soon."

Just then, Clara's phone buzzed again. A text from an unfamiliar number.

"You're getting closer, Detective. But remember, curiosity can be fatal."

Chills raced down Clara's spine. **A threat.** "Mark, I just got another message—" She showed her phone to him, her voice shaking slightly. "It's from someone who knows what I'm doing."

"Turn off your location tracking," he commanded, his tone hardening. "We can't give him any advantages. We need to stay one step ahead."

Clara nodded, her mind racing with the escalating danger. As they strategized their next move, the environment around them buzzed with life—laughter, the clinking of cups, the hiss of the espresso machine—yet Clara felt isolated within an encroaching darkness.

"Let's head back to your office and analyze everything we have," Mark said, glancing around to make sure they weren't being watched. "We need to fortify ourselves before we confront him."

As they were about to leave, Clara spotted a familiar figure at the counter—Zoe, appearing frazzled and scanning the room with wide eyes. Her heart sank. What was she doing here?

"Zoe!" Clara called out, waving her over. "Everything okay?"

Zoe rushed over, her expression a mix of fear and urgency. "I got another message. I didn't know who else to talk to. I think he's trying to find me."

"What are you talking about?" Mark asked, concern etching deeper lines on his face.

"After I spoke to you," Zoe stammered, "I started getting strange messages—people warning me to keep quiet, to forget about the retreat, about Julian. It's like he has eyes everywhere."

"Okay, take a breath," Clara said, trying to maintain calm. "We need to document everything you've received."

Zoe nodded, pulling out her phone. "They're not just threats; they're cryptic, almost like riddles. He's playing a game, isn't he?"

Mark looked between them, his eyes narrowing. "What do you mean?"

"Here," Zoe said, scrolling through her messages. "This one says, *'In shadows and light, secrets take flight. If you seek the truth, beware of the night.'* It's like he's daring us to keep looking."

"Daring us," Clara echoed, her heartbeat quickening. "It's a challenge, isn't it?"

Mark rubbed his temples, considering the implications. "This isn't just a case anymore. He's trying to provoke us, push us into a confrontation. It's as if he wants to test how far we're willing to go."

Clara's eyes lit with determination. "Then we need to accept the challenge on our terms. We can't allow him to control this narrative or intimidate us into silence. If he wants a game, then let's play."

Mark nodded in agreement, his resolve strengthening. "We need to gather our resources, figure out how to turn his challenge into an advantage. We can outsmart him."

"Start digging deeper into the art community—there must be connections, unfinished pieces that could hold clues," Clara suggested, her mind moving rapidly. "And we should uncover anything linked to those messages Zoe received."

As they formulated a plan, Clara felt a surge of adrenaline mix with the fear pooling beneath her skin. They were stepping into an arena marked by shadows—Julian was no ordinary adversary, but a man shaped by art and anguish. Yet they would meet him with determination, ready to turn the game back on its maker.

"Let's move," Mark said, the fire igniting in his eyes. Together, they stepped out of the café, ready to confront the shadows lurking in Julian Mercer's world.

They were now players in a game where the outcome determined life and death, and Clara was prepared to uncover the truth, no matter the cost. The hunt had begun.

Chapter 8: Threads of Deception

The morning light filtered through Clara's office window, illuminating the chaos of papers and photographs that lay strewn across her desk. The names of the victims and the connections they shared loomed large in her mind, intertwining like a web designed to ensnare the unprepared. After meeting with Zoe, Clara felt a sense of urgency to unravel the threads binding Julian Mercer to the grim fate of the three victims.

Mark leaned against the doorframe, arms crossed, a look of concern etched on his face. "You okay? You've been at this for hours."

"I'm fine," Clara replied, suppressing a yawn. "I just can't shake the feeling that we're missing something. Zoe's testimony adds another layer, but we still don't know enough about Julian's movements after the retreat."

"Maybe we need to dig deeper into his past," Mark suggested. "Look into his previous exhibitions or personal life."

Clara nodded, tapping her pen against the desk. "Yeah, but not just that. I want to know how he interacted with the other artists at the retreat. They must have chatted on social media or discussed his work. I'll check if there's a forum or any groups where they might have gathered."

With renewed determination, Clara pulled up her laptop. As she began searching for online threads or forums related to Julian and the retreat, an unsettling reality began to crystallize. The more she learned about Julian, the clearer it became that he had mastered the art of manipulation, effectively weaving a false narrative around himself.

Hours slipped by, and Clara's focus sharpened as she discovered threads that unraveled the fabric Julian had carefully constructed. His previous exhibitions had featured artworks that spoke of loss and madness, yet there were whispers of more sinister themes lurking beneath the surface. Comments from attendees hinted he had a knack for captivating audiences while simultaneously instilling a sense of dread.

"Here!" Clara exclaimed, calling Mark over. "I found a post from someone who attended one of his earlier shows. Listen to this—'Julian's art speaks to the madness within us all, but it feels like he's drawing us closer to the edge.'"

Mark frowned, studying the screen. "That's not just commentary; it sounds like a warning."

"With Julian, every piece seems deliberate," Clara said thoughtfully. "He seduces people—pulls them into his world and keeps them there. We need to find out how many were truly affected by him. Let's look for past participants of his exhibits or retreats."

Suddenly, a thought struck Clara. "What if some of the guests turned against him? If he pushed too far, there might be someone who's ready to talk."

As she continued scrolling, she stumbled across a social media group dedicated to local artists in the community. Clara quickly requested to join, hoping it would connect her to people who might have insight into Julian and his influence.

Minutes later, a notification popped up on her screen. She was approved, and dozens of posts greeted her—artists sharing their work, critiques, and personal experiences. Clara's eyes darted across the screen, searching for mentions of Julian.

"Got one!" she called out. "Listen to this—'After spending time with Julian, I felt both inspired and suffocated. He has a way of making you question everything.'"

Mark leaned closer. "This doesn't bode well. It seems like he wasn't just creating art; he was creating a cult of personality."

Clara nodded, feeling the weight of the revelation settle in her stomach. "We need to track this person down."

As Clara crafted a message to the user, hoping for a response, Mark received a call and stepped outside. The minutes ticked by, and Clara felt the anticipation building within her.

Finally, Mark returned, a grim expression on his face. "We have a problem."

"What happened?" Clara asked, her heart racing.

"It's about Zoe. She's gone. I checked in with her apartment—there's no sign of her. Neighbors said she left in a hurry late last night, but they didn't see where she went."

Clara's pulse quickened as dread washed over her. "Why would she leave? Does she think Julian is after her?"

"Maybe," Mark said, shaking his head in frustration. "We need to find her before it's too late."

Clara felt the familiar knot tightening in her chest. "We'll check her social media—maybe she posted something before she left."

They pored over Zoe's posts, searching for clues, but the usual cheery updates were now replaced with vague allusions to fear and uncertainty. "This one stands out," Clara said, pointing at a post from the previous day. Zoe had captioned a photo of the gallery with the words: "A beautiful façade can hide the darkest truths."

"Do you think she knows more than she let on?" Mark questioned, concern lacing his voice.

"I think we're on the right track," Clara replied, determination igniting in her core. "She must have realized that her connection to the retreat—and to us—put her in danger."

"Let's backtrack," Mark suggested. "Where were the last places she was known to be?"

"Her café was a regular hangout," Clara said, thinking out loud. "And she attended the last exhibit at Fisher's. Let's see if we can find any of her friends or acquaintances there."

"This is getting messier by the minute," Mark murmured as he grabbed his coat. "Let's move."

The streets outside were busy with passersby, but Clara's mind raced with fear for Zoe. The strings of deception that surrounded Julian had ensnared another innocent life, and Clara was determined to cut through them before it was too late.

They arrived at the café to find it quiet, a stark contrast to its usual vibrancy. Clara approached the barista on duty, a young man with a wary expression. "Hi, we're looking for Zoe Campbell. Have you seen her today?"

"Zoe? No, she hasn't been here. I think she may have left town, but I'm not sure why," he replied, shuffling his feet nervously. "I thought maybe she was taking a break after what happened with the murders."

Clara exchanged a glance with Mark, a sinking feeling settling in her gut. "Do you know where she might have gone?"

"I overheard her talking about wanting to get away for a bit, clear her head..." He hesitated but then added, "I also heard her mention the last exhibit and how it felt ominous to her. She said something about the shadows in the gallery."

Clara's heart raced as she recalled Zoe's earlier comments and the hidden meanings tucked among her words. "Thank you, we need to go."

Outside, Clara felt the weight of urgency pressing down as they navigated their next steps. "If Zoe thinks Julian is a threat, she'll likely avoid any place linked to him. But she might still be reaching out to someone."

"Then we need to get to Zoe before she fades into the shadows," Mark said, determination echoing in his voice. "Let's check in with the gallery staff. They might know about other artists from the retreat who have kept in touch with Zoe."

As Clara and Mark approached Fisher's Art Gallery once more, the unmistakable feeling of being watched settled over Clara, twisting her stomach into knots. The gallery loomed before them like a dark fortress, a repository of secrets that had already consumed three lives and threatened to take another.

Inside, the walls seemed to close in around them, shifting with an unseen tension. Clara couldn't help but feel drawn to the array of abstract pieces that hung within. Each one felt like a window into a mind unraveling, but somewhere among the art lay the threads that could unravel Julian's deceits.

"Let's hurry," Mark urged as they began their search. "We need to pull the threads on this tapestry before it disintegrates completely."

Clara's determination flared; she refused to be a passive observer. As they plunged back into the heart of the gallery's shadows, she knew they were standing at the edge of something dark and dangerous—where the line between art, madness, and reality blurred—and the danger was closing in.

Chapter 9: In the Killer's Shadow

The sun hovered low over the horizon, casting long shadows across the city as Clara navigated the winding streets toward the abandoned warehouse where they had traced Julian Mercer's last known activities. The nagging sense of foreboding settled deep in her chest. The clues they had pieced together felt like threads of a noose tightening around the truth—and the truth increasingly felt like a dark entity lurking in the shadows.

The warehouse loomed ahead, its broken windows like hollow eyes staring back at her. Mark pulled up alongside her, casting a glance toward the ominous structure. "You ready for this?" he asked, his voice steady but laced with concern.

"We have to be," Clara replied, gripping the edge of the car. "If Julian is here, we need to confront him. We can't let fear dictate our actions."

As they stepped out and approached the entrance, Clara felt the air thicken with unease. It wasn't just the remnants of the warehouse that gave her pause; it was the lingering scent of dread that seemed to exude from the very walls. She glanced at Mark, who was scanning the surroundings, his usual bravado tempered by caution.

With a deep breath, Clara pushed open the rusted door, the screech of metal reverberating in the stillness like a warning. Inside, the warehouse was a labyrinth of shadows, the flickering remnants of old industrial equipment casting eerie forms on the cracked concrete floor.

"Stay alert," Mark whispered, moving ahead cautiously. Clara followed closely, her heart racing as they ventured deeper into the gloom. The haunting remnants of forgotten machinery loomed like specters, adding weight to their search.

They maneuvered through the clutter, listening intently for any sign of movement or life. Clara's instincts were heightened, the hairs on the back of her neck prickling with an unsettling awareness. Every creak of the floor beneath them felt amplified in the silence.

Then, a sound pierced the stillness—a low, mocking laugh echoed through the shadows, chilling Clara to her core. "Welcome," it called, dripping with sarcasm. "I've been expecting you."

Clara's pulse quickened; she recognized it instantly. "Julian!" she shouted, her voice reverberating against the warehouse walls.

From the shadows emerged a figure, tall and lean, with disheveled hair that fell across his forehead. Julian Mercer stepped into the dim light, an unsettling smile gracing his lips. "Detective Hayes and Officer Reyes," he mused, his tone playful yet sinister. "To what do I owe the pleasure?"

"Cut the theatrics," Clara said, her voice steady despite the rising terror within her. "We know what you've done. The murders—Emma, Maya, Adam. You're responsible."

Julian raised an eyebrow, feigning innocence. "Responsible? Or merely a mirror reflecting the chaos you all carry within yourselves? They chose to dance with darkness, and I only provided the stage."

Mark stepped forward, fists clenched. "You think this is some sort of game? Those people are dead because of you!"

Julian's smile widened, an unsettling glint igniting in his eyes. "Dead? Perhaps. But they were alive, bursting with potential—until they stepped too close to the truth. The truth can be very unforgiving."

Clara felt a surge of fury but held her ground. "You exploited their pain, Julian. You exploited them. Everyone who came to you for help got hurt."

"Help?" he echoed, his voice rising. "What do you know of help? You bury yourself in a world of paper and responsibility, pretending that solving crimes makes you better than me. But I see through your facade, Detective. You're just as broken as they were."

The shadows seemed to close in around them, darkening the space and feeding into the chaos of their confrontation. Clara's mind raced, piecing together the threads of his words. The twisted philosophy that had guided Julian. He viewed himself as an artist, crafting pain into a form of truth—dehumanizing his victims in the process.

"Why did you kill them?" she demanded, fighting back the rising tide of desperation. "What were you hoping to achieve?"

Julian's expression changed, the playfulness melting away to reveal a glimpse of the monster lurking within. "They were too comfortable in their lives, too confident in their skills. I had to show them the fragility of existence, the beauty hidden in despair. Some call it art; I call it liberation."

"Liberation?" Clara spat back, her voice shaking with indignation. "You twisted their souls, and now you mock their deaths!"

Suddenly, Julian's posture shifted, a wild intensity igniting in his eyes. "You don't understand! They were chosen because they could rise, could transcend beyond their limitations. But I offered them truth, and truth can be ugly."

Mark moved slightly closer, determination hardening his expression. "You're sick! You think you're some kind of genius when you're just a coward hiding behind a brush and a canvas."

"Coward?" Julian laughed—a cold, sinister sound. "You're wrong. I wield my pain and transformation like a weapon. I force people to confront their darkness."

In that moment, Clara saw something shift—an echo of desperation mingling with madness. She had to turn the tides, to pull the conversation away from confrontation and into its crux. "You think you've been chosen, but you're nothing but a parasite, feeding off the suffering of others."

Julian's smile faltered briefly before he launched forward, the volatile energy shifting his demeanor. "You think you can judge me? You, who hides behind your badge? You think you're the arbiter of morality? Let me show you what I've created!"

Without warning, he darted into the shadows, vanishing from sight. Clara and Mark exchanged a quick glance, adrenaline spiking as they moved to follow. The layout of the warehouse started to twist like an unfamiliar maze, the walls echoing Julian's deranged laughter.

"Stay close!" Mark shouted as he sprinted after the sound, Clara racing behind him. She felt the weight of the chase—an invisible predator stalking them through the maze of old machinery and broken dreams.

Clara's breath came in ragged gasps, her mind racing. They couldn't let him gain control of this situation. They had to contain him before he slipped further into darkness.

Suddenly, a loud crash reverberated from one corner of the warehouse. Clara skidded to a halt, her instincts screaming. "Mark! Over there!"

They rounded the corner to find a large pile of debris cascading around a shattered installation piece, its jagged edges glinting ominously in the fading light. And there, beneath the debris, Julian lay motionless, his figure obscured by shadow.

"Julian!" Clara called out, edging closer, her heart pounding.

As she neared, he stirred, eyes flickering open, wild and furious. "You think you can cage the darkness? You're too late, Clara! You will never understand what I've created. It's already too late!"

Clara's gaze narrowed as she approached him cautiously. "You can't run from this, Julian. We'll make sure you pay for what you've done. You can't use art as an excuse for murder."

Julian's expression twisted. "You can't kill the truth! The shadows will always be here, hunting you... waiting for you to join them."

In that moment, as the weight of their confrontation hung heavy in the air, Clara felt the shadow of Julian's madness press down on her, blending with her own fears and doubts. The past had come rushing back, echoing through the chaos of their exchange.

But she would not be consumed. **Not again.**

Mark moved forward cautiously, ready to detain Julian. Clara stood resolute, a guardian against the encroaching darkness, knowing the fight for the truth was only just beginning.

Chapter 10: Beneath the Surface

The morning sun spilled through the office window, illuminating the chaos of Clara's workspace. Files overflowed, strewn about like fallen leaves, each page holding fragments of a story yet to be fully understood. She had barely slept, the relentless need to piece together the puzzle driving her deeper into the murky waters of the investigation.

The revelations from Zoe weighed heavy on her mind. Julian Mercer was not just an artist; he was a puppet master, ensnaring the souls of those who crossed his path. Clara had to uncover not just where he was hiding but the darkness that fueled his art, the emotional depths that inspired his sometimes violent expression.

After gathering her notes, Clara set her sights on an intriguing lead: a local art critic who had spoken out against Julian's work in the past. If anyone could provide insight into Julian's psyche, it would be someone who had dared criticize him. She rushed out of the office, determination guiding her footsteps.

The critic's name was Lydia Hart, a well-respected figure in the art community known for her sharp pen and even sharper opinions. When Clara arrived at the small, contemporary gallery where Lydia often held court, she found the atmosphere abuzz with a new exhibit opening. Yet, the moment Clara mentioned her name, the mood shifted.

"Lydia's not taking interviews right now," the assistant said, her eyes darting nervously around the room.

"I understand," Clara replied, trying to maintain composure. "But it's important. I'm investigating Julian Mercer, and I believe Lydia has insight into his past."

The assistant hesitated. "Wait here."

Moments later, Lydia emerged from the crowd, her presence commanding even amidst the chaotic energy of the gallery. She wore a long, flowing dress, her hair wound up in an elegant knot. The spark of brilliance in her eyes dimmed slightly upon seeing Clara.

"What do you want?" Lydia asked, crossing her arms defensively.

"I need your perspective on Julian," Clara said, holding her ground. "I believe he's involved in the murders of three individuals connected to him. You've critiqued his work; you must know something."

Lydia sighed, stepping aside, her features softening just a fraction. "Fine. Let's talk."

They moved to a quieter corner of the gallery, where the din of the crowd faded into a murmur. Clara sensed the tension in the air—every gaze lingering on the latest works, unaware of the shadows lurking just beyond the art.

"I've written extensively about Julian's art," Lydia began, her tone shifting from indifference to something more serious. "At first, I thought it was merely provocative, a superficial attempt to elicit shock. But the deeper I looked, the more I realized it was a mirror of his mind—fractured and chaotic."

"Fractured?" Clara pressed. "What do you mean?"

Lydia leaned closer. "Many artists channel their pain into their work; they create something beautiful from suffering. But Julian—he seemed to revel in it. I've seen his pieces change drastically after emotional upheavals in his life. When he lost someone close, his art shifted to a much darker, more violent expression."

"Did you know who he lost?" Clara asked, interjecting the urgency she felt in her gut.

"A girlfriend," Lydia replied, her voice dropping to a whisper as if the name itself held power. "Her death affected him profoundly. He became obsessed with the idea of capturing grief in its rawest form. I suspect that's when he started losing touch with reality."

Clara felt that familiarity wash over her again—a shadow of her own past. "And what about those involved in the retreat?" she continued. "Were they aware of his history?"

"They were mesmerized, blindly following him down a path that they believed was enlightening," Lydia said, her tone laced with bitterness. "Julian had a way of preying on vulnerability. For some, art is an escape; for others, it becomes a snare. He used their emotions against them, stripping away any sense of protection."

"Do you think he would resort to murder?" Clara asked, her heart racing.

"Art can take on a life of its own, especially one born from pain and anger," Lydia warned. "I wouldn't put it past him. When you tread into the territory of personal demons, one can easily lose their grip on morality."

"Where can I find him?" Clara pressed, feeling desperation seep into her words. "Do you have any idea where he might be hiding?"

Lydia shook her head, distress evident in her eyes. "He rarely shows up in public anymore. I've heard whispers that he frequents abandoned spaces, places that reflect the decay of his mind. Why would you want to confront him?"

"There are lives at stake," Clara insisted, the conviction in her voice firm. "I have to stop him before he claims another."

"Then you'd better be prepared," Lydia warned. "Julian doesn't take kindly to those encroaching on his territory. He views art as a battlefield, and anyone challenging him is a threat."

Clara felt the weight of Lydia's words settle on her shoulders. She was stepping into a realm where reality was painted over with brutality, where art was used as a weapon. "I appreciate your honesty, Lydia. If you hear anything else, please let me know."

As they stepped back into the gallery, Clara's mind swirled with possibilities, and a dark determination settled in her gut. She would have to delve beneath the surface, exposing the shadows lurking there. The shadows that could swallow her whole if she wasn't careful.

A sudden thought struck her—tires squealing, air thick with the smell of oil and neglect. Julian's push and pull with his art had likely spiraled beyond control. As Clara left the gallery, she pulled out her phone to check the locations of abandoned buildings that had once been studios or galleries—places where the boundaries of sanity and art might collide.

She couldn't shake the feeling that Julian was hiding, swirling in the undertow of his own creation, waiting for the next victim to step too close. And she would not be that victim.

The sun dipped lower in the sky, shadows stretching long across the pavement. Clara was racing against time, hoping to find the cracks in Julian's facade before they consumed her whole. But she sensed the darkness encroaching, whispering in the wind, urging her to reconsider—to tread carefully.

But there was no turning back. She was already in too deep, beneath the surface where the true nature of the beast waited, lurking in the depths of his despair.

Chapter 11: Splintered Allegiances

The air was thick with tension as Clara and Mark entered the dimly lit precinct. The hum of fluorescent lights was a constant reminder of the grim reality surrounding them. Clara felt a weight settle in her stomach as her mind replayed Zoe's words. Each fragment of information spun around her thoughts like autumn leaves caught in a whirlwind—connecting, diverging, yet never leaving her.

Mark motioned for Clara to step into the small meeting room at the back of the precinct. The sound of chaos and buzzing voices faded behind them, replaced by an uneasy silence. The room was sparsely furnished—a wooden table surrounded by mismatched chairs, a flickering projector illuminating a white wall.

"Here's what we have," Mark said, spreading out the photographs and notes across the table. "Zoe's revelations tie Julian directly to the victims. Each one felt his influence, his weight looming over them."

Clara nodded, her expression serious. "But it's more complex than that. If he was manipulating them, it suggests they were caught in a web that turned fatal—not just random victims."

Mark rifled through the papers, his brow furrowed. "We need to dig deeper into the retreat's attendees. If Julian created a rift between them, it could explain the motive behind targeting specific people."

"Splintered allegiances," Clara echoed, feeling the truth settle within her. "If Julian fostered divisions, some might have turned on others. Who knows what desperate actions could arise from that chaos?"

Their conversation was abruptly interrupted by the sharp knock of Lieutenant Harris at the door. "Got a minute, Hayes? We need to talk."

Clara exchanged a fleeting look with Mark, then stood to face her superior. "What's going on, Lieutenant?"

"We've got reports about a disturbance near the old warehouse district," Harris said, his tone serious. "There's been word of a possible sighting of Julian Mercer. You both need to head out."

"Right now?" Mark asked.

"Yeah. And it's not just a simple sighting. Sources say Mercer might be involved in something bigger—dealing in stolen art and some underground connections. We need to act quickly."

Clara's heart raced. This could be their chance to corner him, to understand his connection to the threads binding them to the victims. "What's the address?" she asked, already moving toward the door.

Harris handed over a scrap of paper. "Be careful. You two aren't the only ones looking for him. There are others—interested parties that might not play nice."

As they raced towards their car, Clara's mind filled with the implications of this encounter. "Others? Who else is looking for Mercer?"

Mark climbed into the driver's seat, his knuckles gripping the steering wheel. "Criminals? People who lost something in his art world? Or, perhaps, someone who wants to silence him for good."

"Or someone who wants him for their own gain," Clara added, her voice dark with suspicion.

Driving through the city's underbelly, the lights blurred, reflections distorted in the rain-slicked roads. As they neared the warehouse district, the atmosphere shifted. Shadows loomed like reminders of their past, intertwining with the present danger they were racing toward.

Arriving at the warehouse, they parked a couple of blocks away. The structure stood hulking and dimly lit, resembling a behemoth lurking in a forgotten part of town. Clara's stomach twisted with anticipation. "We stick together," she said, her voice steady. "We don't separate. Whatever's inside, it could be volatile."

Mark nodded, unslinging his firearm. "On my count, then."

They moved closer, shadows trailing behind them as they approached the entrance. A flickering light from the warehouse cast eerie shapes across the cracked pavement, illuminating the graffiti covering the aged walls. Clara felt the weight of each step, the significance of what they might find.

Inside, the air was heavy, filled with the smell of decay and something more pungent—fear. The open space revealed scattered crates, remnants of art pieces, fragments of a world turned chaotic. The walls were adorned with half-finished paintings, echoes of beauty consumed by neglect.

"There!" Mark whispered, pointing toward a flickering light from a back room. Clara could make out silhouettes moving—disorderly, hurried, their voices a low murmur.

They crept closer, ears straining to catch fragments of the conversation.

"I told you to be careful! If they find out we're here—" A voice, sharp and frantic, cut through the air.

Clara exchanged a glance with Mark, their breaths held tight. "That sounds like Mercer," she whispered.

"Let's move," Mark replied, stealthily inching forward.

As they neared the room, Clara's heart pounded in her chest. This was the moment. The answers they sought lay just beyond the door, but so did the risk of exposure. Mark carefully nudged the door aside, revealing a small group huddled together, papers strewn about, their expressions tense.

Julian stood among them, his presence commanding, but there was something different in his eyes—a wildness, a desperation. Clara felt a shiver of recognition; this was a man twisted by his own ambitions.

"What do we do?" one member of the group asked, fear etched across his face.

Julian's smile was sharp, devoid of warmth. "We proceed as planned. They think we're finished, but it's just begun. If we can't exploit the darkness, we'll taint the light." His voice was hypnotic, drawing in those around him.

Clara's instincts screamed danger. Mark gestured for her to step back, but she refused. "We can't stay hidden. We need to confront him," she insisted.

"Not yet," Mark urged in a low voice. "We need more information—"

But Clara was already moving, stepping into the light. "Julian Mercer!" she called, her voice slicing through the tension like a knife.

The room froze, eyes snapping to her and Mark, surprise morphing into anger and curiosity. Julian's expression shifted, the chaotic energy suddenly focused on them. "Detective Hayes," he said slowly, a wicked smile creeping onto his lips. "I wondered when you would finally show up."

Mark stepped forward, trying to assert control. "You're under arrest, Mercer. We're not here to play games."

Julian's laughter echoed through the room, unsettling and dark. "Games? Oh, sweet detective, this is only the beginning. You're here just when I need you most. We have unfinished business."

Clara felt the tension escalate. The splintered allegiances among the group reflected in Julian's haunted gaze. "What have you done?" she demanded.

"Everything that needed doing to secure my art, my legacy," he replied smugly. "You think this is about just the victims? You're merely pawns in a game much larger than you comprehend."

Clara glanced around, noting the mixture of fear and loyalty among the group. They were trapped in an intricate web of manipulation, much like the victims before them. "This ends now, Julian. Whatever you're planning, we'll expose it."

The atmosphere shifted, a dangerous undertone infusing the air. The group shifted nervously, glancing at each other as if weighing their allegiances, their loyalties splintering in real-time. Clara could sense the pervasive tension and knew they were on the verge of a breaking point.

"Let's see how far you're willing to go to protect those you care about," Julian sneered. "Because the shadows are always watching, Detective. And I thrive in darkness."

A sudden crash erupted from the back, followed by frantic shouting. Clara turned, heart racing, realizing they had lost their element of surprise. Chaos erupted as the group scrambled, and Clara instinctively moved closer to Mark, determination igniting within her.

"Decide!" Julian shouted, addressing the members of his group. "Will you stand with me, or will you let the light blind you?"

As allegiances strained and fractured, Clara's mind whirled. They were caught in a storm, and the only way out was through the truth. "Mark, we need to get in there now!" she shouted, charging forward, ready to confront whatever darkness lay ahead.

The splintering of allegiances was just the beginning, and Clara was determined to piece together the fragments, even if it meant confronting the shadows of her own past.

Chapter 12: The Masquerade

The grand ballroom of the Montgomery Hotel glittered under a canopy of shimmering chandeliers, casting a golden glow over the elegantly dressed guests, each donned in lavish gowns and sharp suits. Laughter and music mingled in the air, creating an intoxicating atmosphere that belied the darkness Clara Hayes felt lurking just beneath the surface.

Clara stood near the entrance, adjusting her mask, a simple yet elegant affair in black lace that served to conceal her identity but also reflected her tumultuous thoughts. Beside her, Mark Reyes appeared more at ease, his mask a striking contrast of silver and black, complementing his tailored suit. If it weren't for the weight of their investigation pressing on their shoulders, Clara might have even found the setting enjoyable.

"Ready for this?" Mark asked, scanning the crowd.

"Not exactly," Clara replied, her gaze darting around the room. "But Julian is supposed to be here. We need to blend in, gather information, and see if we can find any of his connections."

The masquerade ball was billed as a charity event, ostensibly for the arts, but cloaked in an air of exclusivity that made Clara suspicious. Rumors had circulated that many of the guests had a deeper connection to the art world—people who might turn a blind eye to darker activities in exchange for artistic prestige.

As they made their way through the crowd, Clara felt the prickling sensation of being watched. The masks added an eerie anonymity, imbuing the evening with a sense of deception where no one was who they appeared to be. She glanced at a nearby couple whispering conspiratorially, their eyes darting around as if searching for someone.

"Over there," Mark said, pointing subtly toward a group gathered near the bar. "That looks like members of the artist community. They might know something about Julian."

Clara nodded, her heart pounding. She knew they were stepping onto dangerous ground; connecting with the wrong people could lead them deeper into a web of deceit, but they had little choice. They approached the cluster of guests, their laughter fading as they arrived.

"Good evening," Clara greeted, forcing a smile beneath her mask. "What an extraordinary event, isn't it?"

One woman, her dress a cascade of emerald silk, eyed Clara curiously. "Yes, the gallery's chosen favorites, all in one place. Makes you wonder what else is hidden beneath the surface."

"Indeed," Mark chimed in, his eyes scanning the crowd. "We're hoping to learn more about the artists in attendance tonight. We've heard some interesting things about Julian Mercer."

At the mention of Julian's name, a collective shift rippled through the group. The atmosphere grew charged and tense, the air heavy with unspoken words. The woman Clara had spoken to smirked, her expression filled with disdain. "Ah, Julian. A genius or a menace—depends on who you ask."

"Why do you say that?" Clara pressed, wanting to pry deeper.

"Every artist has their demons," a man chimed in, his face half-hidden behind a half-mask of black velvet. "But he's one of the few who dares to embrace them, which is both thrilling and terrifying. They say he's obsessed with purity in art, to the point of madness."

Clara exchanged a glance with Mark. "Do you know where we might find him tonight?"

Their question was met with silence, the group exchanging furtive glances. The woman finally spoke up, her voice lowered. "Rumor has it he's been sketching at the back of the gallery. Some claim he's working on a new series—depictions of the 'soul' itself."

A shiver ran down Clara's spine. "And what does that mean?"

"Let's just say his last exhibition raised quite a few eyebrows. People speak in hushed tones about how he captures the essence of his subjects. Some say it's like a reflection of their darkest fears," she replied, her gaze unflinching. "I wouldn't go back there if I were you. It's easy to get lost in his world."

"I appreciate the warning," Mark said, his voice steady but cautious. "But we're here to get clarity, not just whispers."

As the conversation flowed, Clara felt the crowd swell with murmurs of excitement. An announcement rang out over the speakers, beckoning the guests to take their seats for the evening's main event. Clara's heart raced at the prospect of confronting Julian.

"Excuse us, please," Clara said, subtly moving away with Mark. "We need to check this out."

They navigated through the thrumming crowd, slipping past clusters of guests until they found themselves at a less crowded corner of the ballroom. A set of double doors adorned with golden handles led to a dimly lit hallway, the kind of passage that felt forgotten amid the pageantry of the event.

"This must be it," Clara whispered, feeling adrenaline surge through her.

They pushed through the doors cautiously, revealing a small room filled with canvases propped against the walls. Each painting was shrouded in darkness, capturing haunting images that evoked deep emotion. In the corner, an easel stood, where Julian Mercer himself bent over a blank canvas, immersed in his work.

"Stay close," Clara instructed, stepping deeper into the room. The air was thick with the scent of oil paint and turpentine, drawing her closer, almost against her will. She fought against the creeping unease that clawed at her insides.

"Julian," Clara called, her voice echoing slightly off the walls. "We want to talk."

He glanced up, his hazel eyes piercing through the dimness, laced with an intensity that sent a chill down her spine. He appeared younger than the stories implied, but there was a timeless quality in his gaze—a darkness that enveloped him.

"Ah, the detective," he replied, a smirk creeping onto his lips, deliberately slow and almost sinister. "To what do I owe the pleasure?"

"Let's skip the pleasantries. We're here about the recent murders," Clara said, her voice firm. "You're connected to the victims."

"Victims... such a strong word," Julian mused, stepping out from behind the easel, his movements fluid and deliberate. "They were my muses, my inspirations. Lovely souls, but often tormented. You should understand that art demands sacrifice."

Mark spoke up, his voice cutting through the charged atmosphere. "What kind of sacrifice? Did you push them too hard? Turn them against each other?"

Julian laughed softly, almost mockingly. "You misunderstand. I don't control their destinies; I merely illuminate the shadows they carry inside. The darkness is where the true beauty lies."

Clara felt her blood run cold. "You're saying they were willing participants in whatever twisted game you played, aren't you?"

"Every artist dances with their demons," he replied smoothly. "But some forget that the true masterpiece is born in suffering. Maya, Emma, Adam—they all sought more from their art; they wished to transcend, to evolve. But not all who reach for the light can escape the darkness."

"Where were you the night they died?" Clara pressed, refusing to back down.

Julian's expression darkened momentarily, but then he masked it with his signature charm. "The world is a complex tapestry, detective. I can't claim responsibility for how threads align or unravel. Art reflects life's impermanence."

A knot formed in Clara's stomach as she processed his words. "You think you're above this, don't you? That you can manipulate souls without consequence?"

Julian's smile widened, but his eyes turned cold. "Ah, but haven't we all been manipulated, Clara? You of all people should know that. Each stroke on a canvas, each hidden desire—it's a masquerade. Who's truly wearing a mask? Perhaps it's you, not me."

The weight of his implication hung in the air, thick as fog. Clara felt the layers of her own history, her own shadows creeping closer, but she pushed them aside, anchoring herself in the moment.

"Enough games, Julian," Mark interjected, his tone sharper now. "We know what's at stake and what you've done. You need to answer for it."

Julian stepped back, the air between them charged with tension. "In the end, it's not me you should fear. Every artist becomes a subject of their own creation. You both tread in waters far deeper than you realize, and the currents can pull you under."

Before Clara could react, a sudden commotion erupted from outside the room. The sound of heated voices filled the hallway, and laughter turned to cries of alarm. Julian's gaze flitted to the door, a mix of interest and amusement flickering across his features.

"Looks like the evening is becoming more entertaining," he said with a mocking lilt. "Perhaps you should join them. Who knows what masks will slip tonight?"

Without thinking, Clara reached for Mark's arm. The sounds of the crowd sparked a new determination within her. She knew they had to push through whatever chaos awaited them outside.

"Julian," Clara called out again, steely resolve in her voice. "This isn't over. We will find out the truth."

His laughter followed them as they rushed back into the ballroom, the masquerade alive and pulsing with an energy that felt both thrilling and ominous.

As they stepped into the fray, the echoes of their confrontation lingered—a haunting reminder of the shadows that could consume anyone who dared to look too closely. In the midst of the celebration, amidst the masks, Clara couldn't shake the feeling: the real danger was just beginning to unfold.

Chapter 13: Requiem for the Innocent

Rain drummed against the pavement, creating a rhythmic symphony that twisted through the night. Clara stood beneath the awning of a small church, its stained glass windows glowing with an ethereal light amidst the deluge. Tonight's gathering was bittersweet, a memorial for the victims who had been taken too soon, where friends and family would come together to honor their memories.

Clara felt the weight of this moment pressing down on her chest. She had spent the past days chasing shadows and leads, but nothing could prepare her for the emotional reminder of the lives lost. Each face, each story, now felt like a puzzle piece in an elaborate, twisted game orchestrated by Julian Mercer.

Mark arrived, hurrying through the rain with an umbrella, his expression somber. "Ready?" he asked, glancing at the gathering crowd.

Clara nodded, steeling herself for what lay ahead. Together, they stepped inside the dimly lit church where flickering candles created a warm yet haunting ambiance.

The congregation, mostly composed of mourners, filled the pews. Clara felt the palpable grief in the air, a silent testament to the lives extinguished too soon. As she moved further in, she spotted Zoe seated near the front, her red hair a stark contrast against the muted colors of her black dress. Clara's heart ached at the sight; she felt a kinship with the girl, both of them haunted by the weight of their shared past.

"Looks like word got out about this," Mark muttered, his eyes scanning the room. "We might have some connections here."

Clara nodded, her gaze falling on a small table draped in white linen. It displayed photographs of the three victims surrounded by candles, flickering flames dancing like spirits above their smiling faces. Emotions swirled through her—anger, sorrow, regret. They hadn't just been victims; they had been vibrant lives, filled with hopes and dreams.

As the service began, the pastor stepped to the pulpit, his voice steady yet filled with compassion. "We gather here today to celebrate the lives of Emma Lang, Maya Tran, and Adam Marsh—a triumvirate of talent, warmth, and kindness. Each of them touched our lives in profound ways, and while their absence leaves an unfillable void, their spirits will forever remain in our hearts."

Clara shut her eyes, allowing the words to wash over her. She could feel the tears welling up, blurring her vision. How many more candles would be lit in memory of lives extinguished by brutality? Her thoughts drifted back to Julian and the darkness he wielded, the manipulation that had led to this tragedy.

"Please take a moment of silence to reflect," the pastor continued, his voice lowering. The room fell into stillness, punctuated only by the soft patter of rain against the stained glass.

As Clara stood in quiet reflection, a ripple of movement caught her attention. Near the back of the church, a figure in a dark coat lingered, the hood obscuring their face. Clara's instincts kicked in; there was something about how they moved, a predatory grace that sent a shiver down her spine.

"Do you see that?" Clara whispered to Mark, nodding subtly toward the figure.

"I do." Mark's voice was low, hinting at alertness. "Let's keep an eye on them."

As the service continued, Clara felt tension building in the air. Her focus drifted between the memorial and the figure, whose posture suggested they were waiting for something—or someone. An unsettled feeling gnawed at her stomach.

When the service concluded, mourners began to rise, and Clara found herself jostled in the crowd as people moved toward the photographs. The figure, however, remained motionless, watching intently.

Clara and Mark exchanged glances filled with urgency. "Stay close," Clara instructed, her voice a whisper steeped in determination. "I'm going to check it out."

Before Mark could respond, Clara slipped into the crowd, weaving her way through the mass of grieving friends and family. The figure, still stationary, finally lifted their head slightly, and Clara's breath caught in her throat.

In the dim lights, she recognized the deep-set eyes and sharp features. It was a face she had seen before—Julian Mercer.

"Clara." His voice had an unsettling calm, almost too serene amid the chaos of mourning. "I didn't expect to see you here."

"Why are you here, Julian?" Clara demanded, refusing to mask the anger simmering just below the surface. "What do you want?"

His lips curled into a subtle smile, deceitful and haunting. "I came to pay my respects," he replied, his tone mockingly genuine. "They were... talented, weren't they? Their art spoke to depths I dared only to hint at."

"Enough," Clara snapped, feeling a surge of rage. "You've taken their lives. You've manipulated innocent people for your own gain. You're not a victim, Julian."

He stepped closer, the shadows cloaking him in an almost ethereal light. "Victim? I'm merely the muse in a story written by others. You forget, Clara, art reflects the creator's soul. Their pain became their masterpiece, and I merely guided them to the canvas of their existence."

"By using them?" she shot back, her heart pounding. "You twisted their pain into suffering. You're a monster."

"Mmm, monsters have many definitions." Julian leaned closer, his voice a mere whisper. "But they also create. Think about it: who truly suffers the most—the creator or the creation? Artists are always at the mercy of their own torments."

Clara felt the walls of the church closing in around her as she struggled to maintain her composure. "You think this is art? Their deaths aren't a reflection of creativity; they're a tragedy!"

"But tragedy is the essence of art," Julian replied, his voice melodic yet chilling. "You'll come to see. You're drawn into the darkness, Clara. Just like them."

Fury ignited within her. "You won't manipulate me, and I will bring you to justice for what you've done."

"I welcome the chase," he said, his eyes glinting with an unsettling enthusiasm. "But remember, dear Clara, the shadows might reveal more about you than you care to admit."

Mark approached, a determined look on his face. "Clara, we need to go. Now."

Julian straightened, the smile never leaving his lips. "I look forward to our next encounter, detective. Trust the shadows. They will guide you."

With that, he turned, slipping away into the crowd, leaving Clara seething with wrath and disbelief. The church felt oppressive, the grief around her becoming suffocating as fresh sobs echoed in the air.

"Are you okay?" Mark asked, guiding Clara toward the exit.

"I don't know," she admitted, her voice trembling. "He's... he's playing with us. With the memories of the people we lost."

Mark nodded solemnly. "We'll stop him. Together."

As they stepped into the rain-soaked night, Clara could feel the weight of the service pressing down upon her. The requiem for the innocent had begun, but it was far from over.

They had work to do, but for Clara, each step forward felt intertwined with the shadows of the past, the echoes of lives lost still haunting her. She had to confront those echoes, face the darkness Julian represented, and find the truth hidden within the tragedy—a truth that might lead to redemption for the innocent, and perhaps for herself as well.

Chapter 14: Psychological Warfare

The tension in Clara's office had reached a boiling point. News of the latest murder had sent shockwaves through the precinct, leaving a trail of unease that clung to Clara like a second skin. A fourth victim, a local art dealer named Richard Galloway, was found dead under eerily similar circumstances—his body hidden among sculptures in his own gallery, a brush in one hand, as if he had been caught mid-creation in a twisted last act.

Clara stared at the crime scene photographs spread across her desk, dark shadows playing across each image. The brutality of Richard's death echoed the previous ones—a violent act disguised as art but undeniably personal. The killer was reaching out to her, taunting her with the artistry of murder.

Mark paced the room, the hardwood creaking under his weight. "It's as if the killer is trying to ensnare you, using the art world against you. What does he want, Clara?"

"I can't be sure," she replied, her voice strained. "But he's manipulating the narrative, playing with each victim's story like a maestro with his symphony. We need to think like him."

Mark stopped, a sense of urgency in his posture. "You're saying we should get into his head? That's dangerous."

"It's our only chance to understand his motive," Clara insisted. "Julian thinks he's invincible, that art grants him permission to destroy.

He's turned this into a grotesque game, and we need to play to win—before he decides to come after us."

As the realization sank in, Clara felt the air grow thick with a sense of looming dread. She wasn't just racing against time; she was wading into a psychological labyrinth where the stakes had never been higher. The killer had turned their investigation into psychological warfare, and if she wasn't careful, she could end up just another victim caught in his web.

"Mark, we need everything we can find on Julian's past," she said, determination lighting her eyes. "His art reflects his state of mind. If we can expose the cracks in his façade, maybe we can anticipate his next move."

Mark returned to her desk, flipping through the documents, his focus shifting to a newspaper article pinned on the board. "Look at this—after his controversial exhibit, he had a major fallout with several friends and fellow artists. And not just that, but his behavior became increasingly erratic. He pulled away from everyone."

"Isolation breeds paranoia," Clara noted, frowning. "He must feel cornered, and cornered animals are the most dangerous. We've seen how he treats those who challenge him."

Mark pointed to a timeline of social media posts and emails. "These interactions suggest he was obsessed with perfection—he demanded it from his work and those around him. What if he sees the victims as flawed representations of his ideal?"

"Or as betrayals," Clara added, her mind racing. "He might see their successes as a direct insult to his suffering. He's leading us down a carefully crafted path that centers around his own twisted narrative."

They both fell into silence, the weight of understanding gluing them to the desk. Clara suddenly straightened, a thought crystallizing in her mind. "What if we invoke his anger? What if we disturb his sense of control?"

Mark raised an eyebrow, questioning her plan. "You're suggesting we provoke him? That could backfire spectacularly."

"We can't afford to play safe anymore. He's too far gone, and if we want to bring him down, we've got to fight fire with fire. We need to give him a scapegoat. Make him believe we're going after someone he views as a rival."

"Someone from his past," Mark said, catching her drift. "Maybe it's risky, but it could draw him out. Who do we have?"

"I remember the woman at the gallery," Clara said, recalling Zoe Campbell's frantic words. "She mentioned other artists from the retreat who had challenged Julian's vision. We can use one of them."

Mark nodded. "Names?"

"We start with Emma's mentor, Claire Dubois. She had strong ties to Maya and Emma. Let's schedule a meeting with her and see if we can provoke a response."

With newfound resolve, Clara and Mark plotted their next moves. They needed to play this psychological game deftly, knowing that their own mental fortitude would be tested. As evening fell, shadows enveloped Clara's office, but they ignited a flicker of determination within her that mirrored the darkness encroaching around them.

THE FOLLOWING DAY, Clara and Mark met Claire Dubois at a modern café overlooking the city's bustling art district. The atmosphere was vibrant, filled with chatter and clinking cups. Clara hoped the lively setting would draw out Claire's emotions and fears—perhaps even provoke a reaction that would lead Julian to slip.

Claire arrived, her presence commanding yet weary. She was in her fifties, with curly silver hair and sharp features that hinted at both wisdom and a hardened edge. Clara introduced herself and Mark, emphasizing their commitment to solving the string of murders within the art community.

"Your students, Emma and Maya—they were extraordinary talents," Claire acknowledged, her voice heavy with grief. "It's a tragedy what happened to them. They had so much potential."

"Thank you," Clara replied, gauging Claire's reactions. "It's crucial we talk about their connections. Julian Mercer has surfaced in some of our investigations."

Claire's eyes narrowed, and Clara noticed a flicker of anger. "That man is a monster. He doesn't deserve the title of artist. He manipulates and destroys."

"Do you think he saw them as threats?" Mark pressed, leaning closer. "As competitors who had surpassed him?"

Claire's fingers tightened around her coffee cup, the porcelain creaking. "Absolutely. Julian couldn't stand the idea that anyone could encapsulate beauty without his oversight. They dared to exist outside his shadow."

Clara seized the opportunity. "Do you think he'd retaliate? Perhaps against any rising talent that challenges his 'vision'?"

The question unsettled Claire. "I wouldn't put it past him. He sees life as a canvas where he's the sole creator. Anyone who detracts from his narrative becomes disposable."

Mark exchanged a glance with Clara, sensing her anticipation. "You know, with everything that's happened, it wouldn't be surprising if he felt cornered. It's like a predator backed into a corner. He could lash out at anyone he perceives as competition."

Claire's gaze sharpened. "What are you implying?"

"If he sees the world as a canvas—and you as a rival—it's a dangerous combination. You've tallied a lot of success, Claire. Perhaps he sees you as the ultimate affront to his delusions," Clara said, pressing the edges of provocation.

Claire's face hardened, her composure slipping. "I have no intention of engaging with someone like him. He's beneath me."

"But he needs a target," Clara pressed. "We think provoking him might bring him out. We could use this to our advantage."

Claire began to shake her head but faltered, her gaze shifting between them. "You're playing a dangerous game. He's unpredictable and delusional. If you provoke him, you have no idea how far he will go."

"We're fully aware of the risks," Mark countered. "But if this tactic leads to his capture, we're willing to try."

The café buzzed around them, but Clara's focus was intently on Claire. As they continued discussing strategies, the walls of psychological warfare began to close in on them, a heavy reminder of how unpredictable their quest had become.

CLARA COULD FEEL THE tension mounting as they left the café, the weight of their plan settling uncomfortably on her shoulders. The balance of power had shifted; they were now players in a twisted game that Julian had orchestrated. Yet there was a sense of purpose behind their actions—a hope that by invoking his ire, they might finally unearth the truth behind the shadows he cast.

As night fell over the city, Clara felt an unsettling calm cling to her. With every move they made, they drew closer to the heart of Julian's dark mind—a descent into a psychological battlefield rife with danger.

But Clara knew that the most potent weapon against an adversary like Julian wouldn't be mere strategy; it would be resilience. She steeled herself, gathering the fragments of hope that remained, ready to face whatever chaos awaited them in the gallery of shadows.

Chapter 15: Fractured Reality

The air was charged with an unsettling tension as Clara stood in front of the cracked mirror in her small apartment. The reflection staring back at her seemed... off. Her dark hair was pulling free from its hastily tied bun, and the dark circles under her eyes told a story of sleepless nights and harrowing investigations. But it wasn't just her appearance that felt disjointed; it was the depth in her own gaze—the haunted look that suggested a mind unraveling under the weight of its truths.

Over the past weeks, Clara had chased shadows, each revelation both a beacon of hope and a potential descent into darkness. Julian Mercer had become an obsession, a specter lurking behind every corner, every decision, woven into her waking thoughts and nightmares alike. The threads that bound her to the victims twisted tighter as she delved deeper into their world, seeking answers that only led to more questions.

The recent events tore at the fabric of her reality. Zoe's revelations at the park replayed in her head like a fractured record, each word a jagged piece of the puzzle. Julian's belief that art was a vessel for suffering—a reflection of the creator's soul—echoed ominously in her thoughts. Clara felt a chill creep along her spine, a sense that understanding the artist might shatter not just the case but something within her.

With a shaky breath, she turned away from the mirror and focused on the clutter of notes spread across her desk. Each piece of evidence pointed toward Julian, yet the further she dug, the more elusive he became. Where was he hiding? What did he truly want? The chase had become a labyrinth where every path felt like a dead end, leading her deeper into a place she feared she might not escape.

Just then, her phone buzzed, startling her. It was Mark: **"Need to meet at the gallery. We've got something."**

The familiar flutter of adrenaline surged through her, pushing aside her anxiety. She quickly grabbed her jacket and headed out, the weight of the night pressing down on her.

At Fisher's Art Gallery, the bright lights illuminated the faces of patrons who wandered through the space, blissfully unaware of the darkness unfolding around them. Clara spotted Mark near a cluster of art pieces, his brow furrowed in concentration as he conversed with a gallery employee.

"Clara!" he called out, waving her over. The urgency in his voice made her heart race faster.

"What's going on?" she asked, taking a deep breath to steady herself.

"We had a lead on Julian," Mark replied. "One of the employees here has been keeping tabs on some suspicious activity." He gestured toward a thin, nervous-looking young man with glasses, who stood shifting his weight from one foot to the other.

"Julian was seen in the area last night," the employee said, wringing his hands. "He was lurking outside, watching people as they left. I didn't think much of it at the time, but then I remembered what's been happening... and...I got scared."

"Did you see where he went?" Clara pressed, feeling the tight knot of urgency in her chest.

"He disappeared before I could get a good look," the employee admitted. "But he was looking at a specific piece—the 'Mirror of Souls.'

It's a recent installation, very dark, very... intense. I mean, I could feel something off about it too, you know?"

"Where is it?" Clara asked, her instincts kicking in. She knew they had to act fast.

"Follow me," he said, leading them toward the darkened corner of the gallery.

As they approached, Clara's heart thumped in rhythm with the soft spotlight illuminating the installation. "Mirror of Souls"—the name alone sent a shiver down her spine. The piece was crafted from various shards of reflective glass, arranged in a sinister collage that seemed to warp and twist perspectives, distorting reality itself.

"What do you think?" Mark whispered, scanning the area for signs of Julian. "Is this his?"

"Definitely," Clara replied, her pulse racing as she stepped closer to the installation. She felt drawn to it—compelled to understand the chaos within its depths. "It embodies everything he believes about art and suffering."

The light flickered, casting distorted shadows on the walls as Clara reached out to touch the surface of the mirror. With each touch, a ripple of unease coursed through her. It was as if the shards were alive, whispering secrets just beyond reach, hints of pain and desire tangled in the glass.

But as she drew closer, her reflection fractured, splitting into multiple versions. Each image caught her gaze—one tired and worn from relentless pursuit, another more vibrant yet shadowed by doubt. A voice echoed in her mind, an unsettling juxtaposition of her thoughts and fears.

"To know the truth is to be consumed by it."

"Clara?" Mark's voice broke through the fog, pulling her back to the moment. "Are you okay?"

She blinked rapidly, shaking off the disorienting spell of the installation. "Did you hear that?" she breathed, her heart racing.

"Hear what?" Mark looked at her with concern.

"The voices... I thought—" Clara shook her head, embarrassed. "Never mind. I just... I felt something."

The employee shifted nervously, glancing between them. "Maybe we should go back. This piece... it's stirring something in you."

Without waiting for permission, Clara moved closer to the artwork. The more she gazed, the more she felt a connection—a pulling sensation that resonated in her bones. "Julian views the world through such a broken lens," she murmured, stepping into the shadows of shattered reflections. "What if understanding his work means unlocking his mind?"

Mark stepped forward, his voice firm. "We need to focus, Clara. If we want to find him, we can't get lost in the art. This isn't just a case anymore. You've seen what obsessions can do—it—"

"Mark!" Clara interrupted, suddenly alert. "What if it is connected? This mirror is a manifestation of Julian's psyche. We need to explore what he feels about the victims—about their deaths."

"I don't think that's a good idea," the employee cautioned, his face paling. "People get lost in their reflections...they see things that aren't really there."

"Exactly," Clara said, her conviction building. "Finding Julian means uncovering the darkness that's intertwined with all of this. Art reflects the truth, Mark. We just have to look deeper."

Mark hesitated but nodded reluctantly, a flicker of understanding crossing his face. "Alright. Let's figure out how this connects back to him."

As they stood before the mirror, an eerie stillness enveloped them. Clara felt her heart race as she peered into the shards, searching for answers beneath the chaotic surface. She focused, determined to connect the splinters of reality that Julian had created.

With each reflection, she glimpsed snippets of the victims' lives, moments filled with laughter, hope, and despair. But the more she looked, the more she sensed an ominous thread weaving through—it was a tapestry of emotion stitched together by Julian's vision.

"Clara, we need to go," Mark said, breaking her concentration. "This isn't safe. We can't afford to get distracted."

But she shook her head, biting her lip as she continued to stare. "Wait... let me just..."

Suddenly, the lights flickered violently, plunging the gallery into momentary darkness. Clara felt a jolt of terror grip her as shadows danced menacingly before her. Then, as quickly as it had begun, the lights returned, illuminating Mark's worried face.

"Clara!" he shouted, grabbing her arm. "We need to leave now!"

But it was too late. The aura around the mirror had shifted, and without warning, Clara was thrust into an intense flood of memories, images crashing over her like a wave, tearing at the fabric of her reality. She was standing in the midst of the retreat, seeing Maya's pain, Emma's struggle, Adam's desperation—all flickering like fireflies before her, illuminating a dark truth.

Julian was there too, a dark figure entwined in their souls, a puppet master pulling the strings of their despair. The sounds of laughter melded into cries, her heart pounding as she tried to discern what was real.

"Art is a reflection," he whispered, his voice echoing in her mind. "But not all reflections tell the truth."

Clara gasped, stumbling back as the reality of what she'd witnessed crashed into her. Pieces of the puzzle had fallen into place, but the clarity she sought was tainted by fear. Julian was not just a killer; he was an artist painting in blood and shadows, and she had unwittingly stepped into his world.

Mark steadied her, concern etched on his face as Clara fought to ground herself. "We need to regroup, Clara. We can't face this alone."

"Wait," she breathed, grasping his arm. "If we know this... we might be one step closer to finding him."

As she spoke, an unsettling truth gnawed at her, reminding her that they were now entwined in a game—a sinister dance with an artist who saw the world as a canvas to be splattered with fear and loss. The line between hunter and hunted was blurring, and Clara realized that understanding Julian might just come at a cost greater than she had anticipated.

Together, they stepped away from the fractured reflections, leaving behind the installation that had whispered secrets into their souls. But the weight of knowledge lingered, haunting them as they plotted their next move in a game where reality itself had become their greatest adversary.

Chapter 16: The Ties That Bind

The sun dipped low in the sky, painting the city in hues of orange and purple. Clara stood at the edge of the rooftop, her eyes scanning the horizon, the weight of the world heavy on her shoulders. Everything had led her to this moment, and yet the pieces of the puzzle still felt frustratingly out of reach. The relentless search for Julian Mercer had turned into a labyrinth—each twist revealing more darkness but fewer answers.

"Clara," Mark's voice broke her reverie as he approached, his expression serious. "I think we need to confront the ties that bind us to this case. Julian's not just a suspect; he's a catalyst. We need to understand his influence over our victims and over others like them."

Clara nodded, fixating on the distant skyline. "I've been going over everything we've learned. Julian's presence looms large over these people—his art, his retreats. It's like he has this hold on them, manipulating emotions and vulnerabilities to fuel his vision."

Mark leaned against the ledge, casting a sidelong glance at her. "And that vision seems to be one of chaos and pain. We need to dig deeper into his background—see what connections he had with each victim beyond the retreat."

Clara turned to him, determination etched in her features. "Let's revisit their stories. Not just their time with Julian, but their lives leading up to it. Something must have drawn them to him, and it might reveal something we're missing."

As the sky darkened, they made their way back down the stairwell, the weight of urgency propelling them forward. In the cramped confines of Clara's office, they spread out all the evidence she had gathered—photographs, articles, notes, and the remnants of the victims' lives that still echoed within the pages.

"Let's start with Maya," Clara suggested, grabbing her file. "She had a complicated relationship with her family, especially her father. He was a former artist himself, but he disapproved of her choices, calling her pursuits frivolous."

Mark nodded, flipping through his notes. "That rejection could have pushed her to seek validation elsewhere. Julian's charismatic approach might have appealed to her need for acceptance—especially if he made her feel like her struggles were valid."

"Right," Clara said. She picked up a photo of Maya at the retreat, a smile stretched across her face. "But what happens when admiration turns to obsession? Is that what Julian preyed upon?"

They moved on to Emma. "She had a life filled with expectations. Her family wanted her to pursue a 'real' career," Mark noted. "Maybe she sought solace in Julian's world, where she could express herself freely."

Clara felt the heaviness of Emma's dreams crushed under the weight of her family's expectations. "That type of pressure can be suffocating. It's no wonder she found Julian's dark and passionate art appealing—he embodied everything she wished to express but felt she couldn't."

"And Adam..." Mark continued, his voice trailing off as he rifled through the notes. "He seemed to have everything, but underneath, he was struggling with deep insecurities. He tried to save Maya, protect her, but it seems his own battles with identity consumed him."

"Connecting these dots brings us closer," Clara said, her thoughts racing. "Each victim found a piece of themselves in Julian, but it also became a dangerous reflection of their inner demons. They were drawn to him, but they didn't realize the threat he posed until it was too late."

The room was thick with silence, the weight of their realizations pressing against them. Clara felt the ghosts of the victims watching, urging them to keep digging. "Mark, did you ever feel like someone was watching you while you were speaking to Zoe? Like there were hidden eyes on us?"

"I did," Mark admitted, frowning. "There's something more at play here. I spoke to some of Adam's colleagues, and they hinted he was involved in something risky—a project that could expose secrets of the local art scene. What if Julian saw that as a threat?"

Clara's heart raced. "Could it be that Adam's investigation into Julian's past stirred something dark within him? Maybe Julian never intended for them to find out anything... Maybe he felt cornered."

"Perhaps," Mark replied. "And if that's the case, we need to find out what Adam discovered. He may have been gathering information that would lead to public scrutiny of Julian, and that could mean he was next on Julian's list."

Clara's thoughts swirled. "If we can trace Adam's steps, we might discover something crucial. We need to dig into his recent projects and see if there's a connection to Julian's art or his earlier works."

As they worked through piles of paperwork, Clara's mind inevitably returned to her own past. She felt a knot tighten in her chest—her own struggles had led her into dangerous territory before. "Mark, do you think we're getting too close? That we might become an extension of whatever toxic energy Julian has wrapped around himself?"

Mark met her gaze, his expression firm. "We can't let fear dictate this investigation. We owe it to Maya, Emma, and Adam to expose the truth. If Julian is the predator we suspect him to be, then staying close to our objective is crucial."

Clara nodded, feeling an innate sense of purpose surge through her. She picked up the file on Adam once again and turned it over in her hands. There had to be a clue, something that could unlock the rest of the puzzle.

"Let's go to Adam's workspace first thing in the morning," Clara decided, the conviction in her voice clear. "We need to piece together what he was working on before it became fatal."

"Alright," Mark said, a hint of reassurance in his tone. "But we have to be careful. We don't know how far Julian's reach goes, especially if he has people watching us."

Together, they moved the scattered papers, attempting to create some order out of the chaos. As Clara worked, the looming shadows of the victims danced at the edges of her mind, each one a reminder of connections, the ties they had shared, and the bond that united them against the darkness.

When the clock struck midnight, Clara felt the weight of exhaustion settle over her, but she pushed through. She glanced at the photos laid out before her; they reflected not just loss but also a fiery tenacity that had drawn them together. Each connection, each story lived out in vivid colors, created a tapestry of tragedy that was waiting to be unraveled.

What had once felt like isolated tragedies had morphed into a collective cry for justice—a call that Clara felt compelled to heed. They would hunt down the ties that bound Julian to his victims and uncover the truth before it was too late.

With a deep breath, she steeled herself for the road ahead, knowing that the darkness was not just something they chased—it was lurking closer, binding itself within the very fabric of their journey.

Chapter 17: The Unmasking

The air inside the abandoned warehouse was thick with tension, shadows dancing unsettlingly on the walls as Clara Hayes and her partner, Mark Reyes, crept through the deserted space. What was supposed to be an evening of unraveling the truth had transformed into a chilling standoff, the stakes higher than ever.

Clara could feel the flicker of dread creeping up her spine, a constant reminder of the danger they faced. They knew Julian Mercer was luring them here, playing a wicked game that had already claimed the lives of innocent people. The message he had sent them was cryptic but clear: ***"Meet me where the art of shadows thrives. You'll find the truth there."***

"You sure about this?" Mark whispered, his voice steady despite the palpable fear around them.

"Not really," Clara replied, forcing a calm she didn't feel. "But we have to confront him. He's the only one who can explain why all of this happened."

They slipped further into the shadows, the faint sound of dripping water echoing in the distance. Broken canvases and discarded paint tubes littered the floor like remnants of past lives, and Clara could almost feel the painful energy clinging to the very air. It was a makeshift gallery, filled with remnants of Julian's twisted artistry—a testament to a fractured mind.

As they reached a large open space, Clara paused, her eyes scanning for any sign of the artist. Dim light filtered through cracked windows, illuminating an array of his unsettling works: distorted figures, haunting scenes of despair, and portraits that seemed to seep emotion from the canvas. Each piece told a story of anguish, begging to be understood.

"Julian!" Clara called out, her voice steady. "We know you're here! We want to talk!"

A ripple of silence followed her call, and Clara's heart raced. It was eerily quiet, the kind of stillness that always precedes impending danger. She stepped further inside, the floor creaking beneath her feet. Mark stayed close, his eyes darting for any movement.

Then, from the shadows, a low voice emerged, slick and resonant. "Ah, Detective Hayes. You've come to witness my latest work of art, I see."

Clara's breath caught as Julian stepped into view, an enigmatic figure shrouded in black, his sharp features accentuated by the soft light. His eyes sparkled with a mix of madness and brilliance, embodying the very chaos they sought to dismantle.

"Julian," Clara said, her voice firm. "We need answers. People are dead because of you."

He chuckled softly, a sound devoid of warmth. "Dead? Perhaps. But isn't that the beauty of creation? The end is merely a different beginning."

Mark stepped forward, his voice steely. "You think this is art? You think taking lives is a form of expression?"

Julian's gaze shifted to Mark, his posture relaxed yet predatory. "Art is subjective, Officer Reyes. It is about exploration, and sometimes exploration leads to... casualties." He gestured dramatically to the artworks surrounding them. "Each canvas tells a story—fragmented souls captured in time."

"Stop hiding behind your art," Clara pushed, her frustration boiling over. "What happened at the retreat? Why did you target Maya, Emma, and Adam?"

Julian paused, his expression shifting from bemusement to something darker, more sorrowful. "They were all so eager to understand their pain, their darkness. I merely... opened the door for them. But not everyone is prepared for what lies beyond."

Clara took a cautious step closer. "You cultivated their suffering. You made them vulnerable, and when they didn't meet your twisted ideals, you resorted to violence."

His smile twisted into a grimace. "Violence? No. I merely set them free. They wanted to understand art at its core, and their souls required cleansing."

"Cleansing?" Mark spat, anger flashing in his eyes. "You call murder cleansing?"

"Art does not exist without sacrifice!" Julian's voice echoed in the emptiness, transforming from calm to fervent. "You wouldn't understand. You are shackled by your mundane existence, blinded by the trivial. They sought enlightenment, but in the end, their souls were too weak to endure the truth."

Clara felt a chill sweep through her. "And did you think you could take their lives and call it art? Call it a gift to the world?"

"They were my greatest masterpieces," he crooned, stepping back to reveal a series of portraits looming in the shadows—larger-than-life images of Maya, Emma, and Adam. Their faces contorted in anguish, depictions of death and despair that felt piercingly alive.

Her stomach twisted at the visual cruelty, the grotesque mockery of their memories. "You're sick!" Clara shouted, tears blurring her vision. "You've twisted their suffering to glorify your own."

"Glorify?" Julian laughed, a sound that echoed off the walls. "You misunderstand. I've immortalized them. In their pain lies their beauty. You stand before a legacy!"

At that moment, Clara caught Mark's eye, and they silently communicated. They needed to bring this to an end. It was time to unmask the artist behind the sinister canvas.

"Julian, this ends now," Clara declared, stepping even closer, her voice steady. "You may see yourself as a creator, but you're nothing more than a coward hiding behind your art. You stole their lives, and for that, you will pay."

With a sudden movement, Clara reached into her pocket, revealing the handcuffs she had kept ready for this very moment. As she lunged forward, Julian's eyes flared with a mixture of surprise and rage. In an instant, he dodged, his movements graceful yet serpentine, and Clara felt her heart race.

"Do you truly think you can capture me?" he hissed, a glimmer of manic energy illuminating his features. "You can't grasp the art within the shadows!"

Mark moved to block Julian's route, but the artist was too quick, darting between sculptures and canvases, his laughter echoing off the walls. "You're too late, detectives! This is just the beginning!"

Clara followed him, adrenaline surging, determination fueling her pursuit. They dodged between the grotesque artworks, Clara's breath coming in quick bursts as she tried to anticipate his next move.

"Julian!" Mark shouted, his voice authoritative. "Stop running! You can't escape justice!"

But Julian only laughed, a sound like shattered glass, spiraling into madness. "Justice? Justice is an illusion! It's the law of art that prevails!"

Suddenly, Clara spotted a flicker of movement from the corner of her eye as Julian leaped toward the edge of the warehouse. A familiar figure loomed in the darkness—the woman with hazel eyes, the one from the gallery. She emerged from the shadows, blocking Julian's exit.

"Enough!" she commanded, her voice resonating powerfully. "This ends now, Julian. You can't hide behind your delusions anymore."

Julian halted, confusion mingling with fury. "You dare interfere? You are part of this horror as well!"

"I'm part of stopping it," she replied, her voice steady, bravery radiating from her. "You've twisted art into a weapon, and I won't allow you to harm anyone else."

Clara seized the moment, turning toward Julian, her handcuffs at the ready. "You're done, Julian! You can't manipulate lives any longer."

With desperation surging in his eyes, Julian took a step back, assessing his options. But there was nowhere left to escape. Clara lunged forward, her instincts taking over. In one swift movement, she enveloped his wrists with the cold metal cuffs, locking him into place.

"Julian Mercer, you're under arrest for the murder of Maya Tran, Emma Lang, and Adam Marsh," she declared, steadying herself against the weight of her fears and memories. "You're going to face justice—not art."

His laughter faltered, turning to a menacing scowl as he was led away, bewilderment overtaking him. "You think this is justice? You're all part of the masterful creation—an audience to my truth. But you're too blind to see it!"

As Mark called for backup and shackled Julian to prevent further escape, Clara faced the myriad of twisted faces that surrounded them. They were no longer mere portraits; they were a painful reminder of lost souls, forever intertwined in a tapestry she had vowed to bring to light.

As the flashing lights of police vehicles illuminated the scene, Clara felt an unexpected mixture of emotions flooding through her—a sense of resolve, bitterness for the lives lost, but above all, relief. The unmasking of the killer was not just about capturing Julian; it was reclaiming the narratives of those who had suffered.

Out of the shadows and into their memory, Clara knew their story wouldn't end here. And as she stepped into the darkness of the warehouse, the flickering art around her transformed—what were once grossly distorted images now felt like haunting echoes of strength.

They had faced the darkness together, and together, they would ensure that the true beauty of these souls lived on, shining brightly against the shadows.

Chapter 18: The Last Stand

The air in the abandoned warehouse hung heavy with dust and tension, filled with a silence that felt oppressive. When Clara Hayes and Mark Reyes entered, the shadows danced menacingly around them, as if the very walls were alive, holding secrets of their own. They had received a tip about Julian Mercer's location—a tip that had led them here, to this forsaken corner of the city where broken dreams went to die.

"Keep your guard up," Clara said, her voice a low whisper. She clenched her service weapon tightly, her senses heightened. Every creak of the floorboards echoed in the emptiness, a reminder that they were intruders here, intruding upon the shadows of someone else's turmoil.

Mark nodded, glancing around as they stepped deeper into the warehouse, the dim light filtering through broken windows, casting long beams that illuminated patches of the grimy floor. The place smelled of decay, of memories long dead. Clara scanned the surroundings, her heart pounding with anticipation and dread.

"Where do you think he is?" Mark asked, his demeanor tense.

"I don't know," Clara replied, her mind racing with a mix of thoughts. "But if he's here, we need to be careful. He'll be unpredictable."

They reached a large, open area in the center of the warehouse, cluttered with discarded art supplies—canvases filled with dark images, splattered paint cans, brushes in various states of decay. Each piece was a fragment of Julian's mind, and she could feel the weight of his obsession pressing down on her.

"Is this...?" Mark began, staring at a particularly grotesque painting hanging precariously on the wall.

"His work," Clara confirmed, stepping closer to examine it. The painting depicted a chaotic swirl of colors forming the outline of distorted figures, faces twisted in anguish. It echoed her previous encounters with Julian's art—a reflection of torment and turmoil. "It's like he poured his pain into every brushstroke."

"Clara," Mark said suddenly, his voice tense. "Look."

She turned to follow his gaze toward a dimly lit back room, where the flicker of a candle flickered faintly, casting eerie shadows across the floor. A strange sound echoed from within—a low hum, almost melodic, as though someone was singing softly.

"We need to move," Clara whispered, fear igniting a sense of urgency in her gut. "This way."

As they approached the door, the melody grew clearer, a haunting refrain that sent chills down Clara's spine. She pushed the creaking door open just a crack, peering inside. The sight before her was both beautiful and chilling.

Julian Mercer sat at an easel, brush in hand, surrounded by canvases covered in manic brushstrokes. His eyes were wide, almost feverish, as he chanted a broken melody under his breath. The man appeared disheveled, his clothes stained with paint and dirt, his hair unkempt as he lost himself in the art around him.

"This is it," Mark breathed, his grip tightening on his weapon. "We need to bring him in."

"Wait," Clara urged, gripping his arm. "Let's listen first. We need to understand what he's doing."

Julian's voice, filled with emotion, broke through the silence. "Art is purgation!" he shouted suddenly, the intensity of his passion palpable.

"To create is to purge the soul! They didn't understand! It's not just a reflection; it's a rebirth!"

Clara's heart raced. This was it; this was the man whose twisted vision had shattered lives. The sound of footsteps echoed behind them, and Clara turned to see a shadow at the entrance of the room. Her breath caught in her throat—the figure was Zoe, looking pale and desperate.

"What are you doing here?" Clara hissed, fear gripping her.

"I had to—he needs to know I came back," Zoe pleaded, her voice shaky. "He didn't mean to hurt anyone. He just... got lost in his own pain."

"Lost?" Clara shot back, her frustration boiling over. "He killed them, Zoe! He's dangerous!"

Before Zoe could respond, Julian abruptly turned, sensing their presence. His eyes locked onto Clara, a wild spark igniting within their depths. "You've come to witness my masterpiece!" he proclaimed, a manic smile spreading across his face.

"Julian!" Clara shouted, stepping forward. "You need to stop this! There's still time to make this right!"

He let out a bitter laugh, dissonant and chilling. "Right? You think any of them understood my vision? They were mere reflections, shadows in my art! They had to be sacrificed for the beauty of the true creation!" His voice crescendoed, echoing against the warehouse walls.

"Julian!" Mark interjected, stepping beside Clara, weapon drawn. "You're surrounded. There's no way out of this. Put down the brush and come quietly."

In a flash, Julian's demeanor shifted; the joyful artist was replaced by a furious predator. "You think you can judge me?" He swung around, grabbing a nearby palette knife, his eyes blazing with revenge. "You're all just specters haunting the gallery of shadows!"

"Julian, don't!" Clara shouted, stepping forward, her own weapon drawn. "We can help you. You don't need to do this."

He laughed again, a wild, unhinged sound. "Help? You want to help? You don't understand! This is my art! My liberation!"

In an instant, he lunged forward, his knife glinting in the dim light. Clara's instincts kicked in, and she moved to intercept him, but Mark was quicker. He shot a warning shot into the air, the sound reverberating through the warehouse like thunder.

"Back off, Julian!" Mark barked, using his authoritative presence to remind the artist of the gravity of the moment.

Julian hesitated, his expression flickering between defiance and fear, eyes darting between Clara and Mark, revealing the cracks in his bravado. "You don't know what it means to create! To feel!"

"We understand more than you think!" Clara shouted back, her voice steady despite the chaos in her heart. "We've seen what your art does to people. It consumes them. It's not freedom—it's a prison!"

For a moment, Julian faltered, the knife wavering slightly in his grip. Clara took another step forward, lowering her weapon just enough to show him that she wasn't a threat. "Julian, this doesn't have to end in violence. You have the choice to stop this. You can tell us the truth instead of hiding behind your creations."

His eyes searched hers, and she could see doubt flickering in the depths of his mind. "You think I can walk away from this?" he hissed, suddenly defensive again.

"Not if you keep doing this," Clara said, meeting his gaze with fierce determination. "But you can walk away from the darkness. You can face your demons and let go of the past. You can still create, but not at the expense of others."

There was a stillness for a few heartbeats, the tension thick enough to slice through. The flickering candlelight cast eerie shadows, making the room feel haunted by ghosts from the past—the faces of Maya, Adam, and Emma staring back at them in Clara's mind, their lives extinguished.

Finally, Julian's breath came out in ragged gasps, and the knife trembled in his hand. "They thought they could understand me... But they didn't." His voice cracked, a fissure of vulnerability breaking through his manic façade.

In that moment, Clara saw the man beneath the artist—lost, broken, and terrified. "You can still tell your story, Julian. Just not like this."

With a cry of despair, he dropped the knife, falling to his knees as the weight of his actions crashed down around him. All the rage and pain poured from him, and Clara took a step forward, feeling the air change as she extended her hand toward him.

"Let us help you," she repeated, her voice softer now. "But you have to let go of this anger."

Julian looked up, tears mingling with the paint on his face. "I didn't want it to end this way. I just wanted them to see. I wanted them to—" His voice faltered, collapsing under the weight of his own madness.

Mark moved forward cautiously, holstering his weapon. "Help is here, Julian. We're not your enemies."

As Clara knelt beside him, she knew the journey ahead would be long and fraught with pain. But in that moment of vulnerability, she sensed a glimmer of hope. In the darkness, they could still find a way to heal.

As Julian sagged against the floor, sobs wracking his frame, the shadows began to recede, replaced by the flickering light of possibility. They had faced the abyss and emerged with a flicker of humanity shining through.

But the scars of the past would remain, lingering in the edges of their consciousness, reminders of battles fought and lives lost. In their last stand, they had not only confronted a killer, but they had also illuminated the path toward redemption.

And with that, the art of healing had only just begun.

Chapter 19: Shattered Reflections

The rain lashed against the windows of the old warehouse, creating a rhythm that matched the turmoil within Clara's mind. Deeper shades of night settled over the city, cloaking it in mystery and dread. The confrontation with Julian Mercer loomed ahead, and despite her resolve, fear twisted in her gut. She knew they were close—too close for comfort—and what lay ahead was uncertain.

Clara sat in the back of the dimly lit interrogation room, her breath steadying as she focused on the flickering overhead light. Mark stood beside her, going over the plan one last time. They had invited Julian under the guise of an interview, a necessary step to understand the psychological turmoil that had led to the tragic deaths of the three victims.

"Are you ready for this?" Mark asked softly, glancing at her. His concern was palpable, and Clara appreciated his unwavering support. "We don't know how he'll react."

"I have to be ready," Clara replied, her voice low and determined. "If he gets defensive, we need to keep him talking. Every word he says could uncover something we don't yet know."

Just then, the door creaked open, revealing Detective Coleman, a tall man with a stern expression. "We've got him," he announced. "Let's do this."

The room fell silent as they all turned their attention to the doorway. Julian Mercer entered, a tall figure draped in an oversized coat, his eyes hidden behind dark glasses despite the late hour. He moved with an unsettling grace, the remnants of his artist persona evident even in the confines of the police station.

"Detective Hayes," he greeted, his voice silky, almost mocking. "I didn't think you'd be the one to seek me out."

"Let's cut to the chase, Julian," Clara replied, her voice steady as she gestured for him to take a seat. She could feel the weight of his gaze as he settled across from her, the room thick with tension.

"Fascinated by my work, are you?" he inquired, a sly smile curving his lips. "I've often wondered about the minds of those who create. What compels them? What drives them to insanity?"

"That's precisely what we want to discuss," Mark interjected, leaning forward. "Your connection to Maya, Emma, and Adam. The night at the retreat—their deaths."

Julian's smile widened, an unsettling clarity glinting in his eyes. "Such sensitive souls they were," he mused. "Each a reflection of their own struggles. My art illuminated personal demons that were often left in the dark."

Clara felt her gut clench at his words. "But you took it too far, didn't you? You led them into a web of manipulation. You mocked their vulnerabilities."

His demeanor shifted slightly, a flicker of annoyance passing across his face. "Manipulation? No, I merely revealed truths they were too afraid to confront. I did them a favor by peeling back the layers. Isn't that what we, as artists, are meant to do?"

"Favor?" Clara spat, her frustration bubbling to the surface. "You showed them their pain, but at what cost? They're dead, Julian! Three innocent people whose lives you disrupted for your own twisted vision."

For a fleeting moment, something resembling guilt shadowed his eyes, but it was quickly replaced by a cold detachment. "In the act of creation, one must be willing to sacrifice the weak. Art demands honesty, and not all can withstand the truth," he countered, his tone chilling.

Clara leaned in, refusing to let his words assault her conviction. "And what truth do you believe they uncovered that night? Were you trying to push them into an abyss? Are you the one who took their lives?"

His laughter was low and dark, resonating in the small room like a haunting echo. "You misunderstand the essence of art. I didn't take their lives. I showed them how fragile existence truly is. They were consumed by their own reflections—by their failures, their fears."

The pieces started clicking into place in Clara's mind. "So you admit your influence over them. You led them down this path of darkness, Julian. Why else would they end up like this?"

"I opened their eyes to the truth," he argued, anger flaring behind his calm facade. "Maya's struggle was evident. The moment she walked into my presence, I could see her pain. It was intoxicating."

Mark interjected, his voice rising, "So you decided to break her? How long before you do the same to others?"

Julian's smile remained, but there was a different edge to it now—a challenge. "That's the beauty of creativity, dear detectives. You can't break the unbreakable. True art lives on, even among the shattered remnants. They weren't strong enough to handle what they sought."

Clara felt a surge of rage. "Or maybe you're just a coward hiding behind your art, using it as a weapon to attack the weak."

At that, Julian leaned forward, his eyes narrowing into slits. "Be careful, Detective. This world is but a mirror, reflecting back the truths we dare not face. The weak will always fall. They were merely fragments of my larger canvas."

"Shattered reflections, you mean?" Clara shot back, her heart racing. "You've twisted what it means to create, delving into darkness that you can't escape from yourself. But it'll catch up to you—especially after what you've done."

A shadow crossed his face, a fleeting glimpse of vulnerability before he masked it beneath arrogance. "You think this is over? This is only the beginning. They may be gone, but their legacies? They will haunt you."

Clara could feel the walls closing in, the weight of Julian's twisted perception wrapping around her like a noose. Yet she held onto her conviction; she couldn't let his words — his malignancy — taint her resolution.

"Your time is up, Julian. This ends now," she said with finality, drawing strength from the memories of Maya, Emma, and Adam—the fragility of their lives making each word sharper.

The door swung open, disrupting the tension, as Detective Coleman entered with a few officers. "It's time to take you in, Julian," he declared, stepping towards him. "We're done with the shadows."

As they cuffed him, Clara felt a shiver of relief coursing through her. Somehow, they'd outmaneuvered him. Yet, as she watched Julian smirk, she realized this encounter had opened more questions than it answered. The shadows didn't just belong to him; they lingered within her, too.

"Detective Hayes," Julian called over his shoulder as he was led away. "Remember, we are all merely reflections of the darkest parts of ourselves. Don't be surprised when those shadows chase you, too."

The door swung shut, leaving Clara and Mark in the echoing silence of the interrogation room. The weight of what they had uncovered lay heavy on her heart. Though they had captured Julian, the haunting truth remained—sometimes, it was not just the existence of darkness that defined them, but the reflections it left behind.

As the rain continued to pour outside, Clara felt the remnants of her past stir, shadows whispering their truths. The fight was far from over, and she steeled herself for whatever lay ahead, knowing that understanding her own shattered reflections would be just as pivotal as pursuing justice for the victims.

Chapter 20: Fragments of Truth

The morning sun filtered through the drawn curtains of Clara's office, casting a soft glow over the remnants of the chaotic investigation that had consumed her life for far too long. The air felt lighter today, but the weight of the past still lingered, a constant reminder of the lives lost and the darkness they had faced. Clara sat at her desk, a collection of files, photographs, and notes laid out before her like a fragmented puzzle waiting to be solved.

In the aftermath of the confrontation with Julian Mercer, Clara had spent countless hours sifting through the details. The court proceedings were now over; he had been found guilty of multiple counts of murder, manipulation, and conspiracy. Justice had been served, but it felt hollow, like the echoes of a storm that had quieted but left destruction in its wake.

Clara glanced at the thick case file sitting at the corner of her desk. Inside lay the stories of Emma Lang, Adam Marsh, and Maya Tran—each one a vivid reminder of their struggles, their passions, and their untimely deaths. Each a reflection of the fragments of human experience, caught in the cruel web of ambition, betrayal, and loss.

As she flicked through the pages, her thoughts drifted to the moments leading up to the final confrontation with Julian. She could still hear his chilling laughter, the way he had taunted her with the truth behind his twisted ideology on art and suffering. The gallery of shadows had revealed itself in full, a collection of his dark psyche laid bare before the world, and she had fought through the depths of her own darkness to expose it.

The phone rang, jolting Clara back to the present. She hesitated, glancing at the caller ID before answering. "Clara Hayes."

"Detective, it's Mark," her partner's voice came through, a familiar comfort amid the storm of her thoughts. "I just got off the phone with Zoe. She's been doing a lot of thinking since all of this went down."

"Is she alright?" Clara asked, a wave of concern washing over her. Zoe had played a crucial role in unraveling the mystery surrounding Julian, and the weight of the aftermath had been heavy on her.

"She's doing better," Mark replied. "But she wanted to share something important with you—something about a piece of art Julian had at the retreat."

Clara lifted her chin, intrigued. "What is it?"

"Apparently, he created something that no one has seen since he disappeared. Zoe believes it might hold the answer to everything—the key to understanding his motivations."

Clara's heart raced at the prospect. "I need to meet her. Where can I find her?"

"Let's meet at the café where you first spoke to her. She seemed really eager to discuss this." Mark paused before adding, "I think she's onto something, Clara. It may be what we need to finally put this chapter behind us."

After hanging up, Clara grabbed her jacket and headed out. Despite the sense of closure that had followed Julian's trial, a part of her still felt fragmented—like a puzzle with missing pieces. She hoped Zoe's revelation might just lead her to those final pieces.

The café bustled with the morning crowd, the aroma of fresh coffee and baked goods wrapping around her like a warm embrace. Clara spotted Zoe at a corner table, her fiery hair a vibrant splash against the muted tones of the café. Clara approached, her heart swelling with empathy.

"Hey, I'm glad to see you," Clara said, settling into the chair opposite Zoe. "Mark says you have something important to share."

Zoe nodded, her hands shaking slightly. "I've been thinking a lot about that retreat and Julian. I can't shake the feeling that he didn't just create art for himself. It was like... like he was crafting a narrative, one that involved all of us."

"What do you mean?" Clara leaned in, captivated by Zoe's intensity.

"There was this one piece—an installation he never completed. He called it 'The Canvas of Souls.' He had this wild idea of capturing the essence of each participant's pain and twisting it into something beautiful. It was like he was trying to control the narrative of our lives through art."

"Control?" Clara echoed, thoughts racing. "You think he used your pain against you?"

Zoe swallowed hard, her eyes glistening with unshed tears. "Yes. He would ask us to draw on our darkest experiences, and then he would take everything we shared and twist it. I haven't seen it, but I heard him speak of it—he planned to unveil it at the next exhibit."

"Did you tell anyone about this?" Clara asked, the urgency in her voice rising.

"No," Zoe admitted, her face reddening. "We were all so wrapped up in what he said. At first, it felt liberating. But afterward... I realized he was distorting our truths."

"Where is this installation now?" Clara pressed.

"I don't know," Zoe replied, wringing her hands together. "But I think it might've been left behind at the retreat. If we can find it, maybe we can truly understand what brought all of this about."

Clara felt a flicker of hope, paired with a deep sense of foreboding. "If we could find that installation, it could provide us with insight into Julian's mind—maybe even closure for the families of the victims."

"I'll help you look," Zoe said, a fierce determination glinting in her eyes. "We owe it to them."

Clara nodded, feeling the weight of her resolve settle in. Together, they would confront the shadows one last time.

As they left the café, Clara felt an unfamiliar lightness accompany her. The fragments of her past began to coalesce into a clearer picture, one that promised a confrontation with not just Julian's demons, but her own.

They made their way back to the retreat where it all had begun, a place cloaked in the memories of pain and creation. The sun dipped low in the sky, casting elongated shadows that danced alongside them, a reminder of the darkness that still lurked.

The atmosphere grew heavier as they arrived, the remnants of the installation lingering like ghosts in the air. Clara took a deep breath, steeling herself for what lay ahead.

"Let's see what we can find," she said, leading the way into the dilapidated building that had once been a sanctuary—and now felt more like a tomb.

Inside, the echoes of laughter and creativity felt layered with sorrow. Clara and Zoe moved through the space, searching for signs of Julian's work. As they stepped into a large room marked with remnants of scattered canvases and abandoned easels, something shifted in Clara's gut.

"There!" Zoe pointed to a shadowed corner. A large tarp draped across a structure loomed ominously, barely visible in the dim light.

Clara nodded, her heart racing as they approached. "This must be it."

With trembling hands, they pulled the tarp away, revealing a massive canvas covered in a chaotic swirl of colors. As the light hit it, Clara felt the air grow still, her breath catching in her throat.

The painting was ominous, depicting anguished faces intertwined with grotesque forms—each brushstroke capturing an essence of suffering, yet somehow beautiful in its rawness. For a moment, she felt overwhelmed by the weight of histories captured in each hue—struggles, triumphs, and pain woven together into a tapestry of existence.

"Look closer," Zoe urged, her voice barely a whisper.

Clara stepped forward, her eyes scanning the depths of the painting. As her gaze wandered over the chaotic masterpiece, she felt an unsettling sense of recognition. Hidden among the swirling forms were the faces of Emma, Maya, and Adam—captured within the vortex of color, their souls seemingly trapped yet eternally alive within the artistic chaos.

"Oh my God," Clara gasped, tears welling in her eyes. "This is their truth. Julian didn't just capture their pain; he consumed it."

Zoe stepped back, her expression mingling sorrow and anger. "This is what he wanted. To own their stories, to twist them into something that served his vision."

Clara tore her gaze away from the canvas, her heart pounding with realization. "But we can expose this. We'll show the world how he intertwined their lives, how he preyed on their vulnerabilities."

Zoe nodded, determination shining through her tears. "We owe it to them—to tell their stories."

With newfound resolve, Clara took out her phone, capturing images of the masterpiece that represented so much more than art. It was a testament to the dangers of obsession and the fragility of the human spirit.

As they stepped back, the shadows around them felt less ominous. In that moment, surrounded by the remnants of suffering and echoing stories, Clara understood that they were not just fragments of the past. They were a mosaic of truths longing to be shared, promising to illuminate the path forward.

With their mission clear, Clara and Zoe made their way back, ready to confront not just the world's darkness but also their own. **Fragments** of truth would build a new narrative, one forged from healing, understanding, and the unyielding light of a collective memory.

And as they embraced the journey ahead, Clara felt the past finally begin to settle, no longer a haunting specter but a foundation upon which to build something entirely new.

Don't miss out!

Visit the website below and you can sign up to receive emails whenever Walter Moon publishes a new book. There's no charge and no obligation.

https://books2read.com/r/B-A-AXVLC-JORFF

BOOKS 2 READ

Connecting independent readers to independent writers.